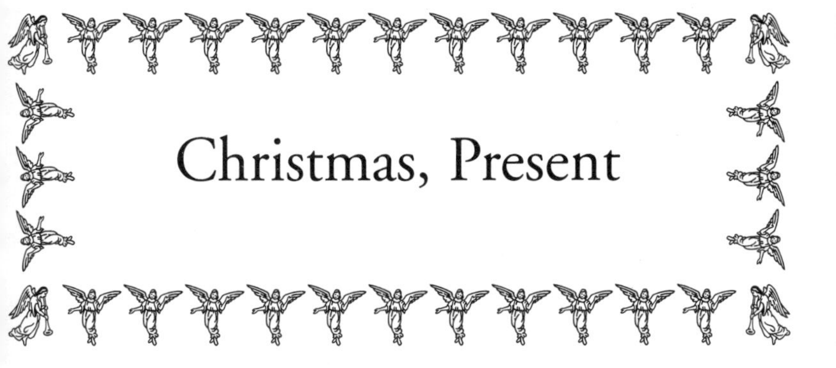

# Christmas, Present

ALSO BY JACQUELYN MITCHARD

*Twelve Times Blessed*

*A Theory of Relativity*

*The Deep End of the Ocean*

*The Rest of Us*

*The Most Wanted*

# Christmas, Present

*Jacquelyn Mitchard*

HarperCollins*Publishers*

 For information, address HarperCollins Publishers Inc., 10 East 53rd Street, New York, NY 10022.

HarperCollins books may be purchased for educational, business, or sales promotional use. For information, please write: Special Markets Department, HarperCollins Publishers Inc., 10 East 53rd Street, New York, NY 10022.

FIRST EDITION

*Designed by Kimba Baker-Feketé*

Printed on acid-free paper

Library of Congress Cataloging-in-Publication Data

Mitchard, Jacquelyn.
Christmas, present / Jacquelyn Mitchard.—1st ed.
p. cm.
ISBN 0-06-056557-8
I. Title

PS3563.I7358C47 2003
813'.54—dc21 2003047816

03 04 05 06 07 ❖/RRD 10 9 8 7 6 5 4 3 2 1

*For the two Karens*

*And for Jill, who read this for pleasure*

# Acknowledgments

Great thanks to my beloved cousins—the few, the odd, the Mitchards—and the days and nights in Tuscany that inspired this story. And to my family, who endured the snowy, terrifying night on the Big Dig that set the stage. And, as ever, and forever, I am nothing without Jane, Patti, Marjorie, and Cathy, muses of all work.

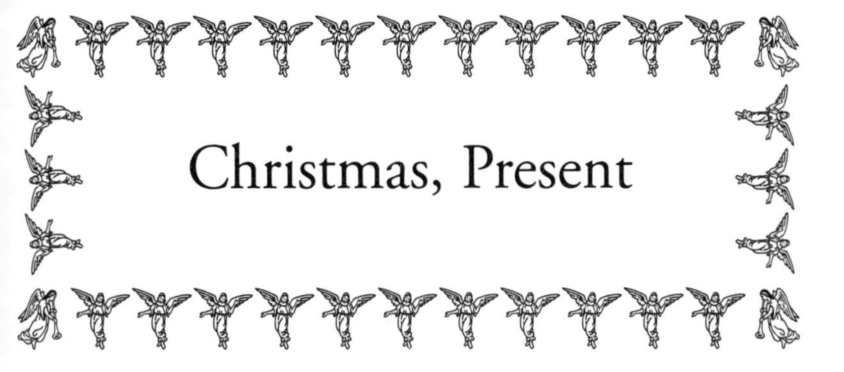

# Christmas, Present

For weeks, he'd pestered himself over the fact that he couldn't remember whether this anniversary was the fourteenth or fifteenth. He would later regret the silliness, the mulling. He might have spent more time with the girls, taken the week off from work, made enormous resolutions and gestures of consummate intimacy.

Still, even in hindsight, a fourteenth anniversary sounded routine, neither a rung on the ladder midway toward a golden sunset nor an observation blushingly fresh and new.

A fourteenth anniversary, like, perhaps, a forty-second birthday, didn't seem to demand so much commemoration.

But one more year would be a landmark! Somehow, to have survived in relative peace and periodic delight for a decade and a half—through the arid, sandy-eyed numbness of sleep deprivation after the girls' births, the unexpected and brutal death of his mother, the long, anxious week waiting for the results of the withdrawal of a microscopic bite of tissue from Laura's breast, Annie's meningitis (ten days during which neither of them finished a single meal, together or separately)—seemed to confer a certain status on this marriage. A marriage of substance, which few of their friends could boast. Fifteen years of marriage in full would cry out for a slam-bang celebration. A high school reunion equivalent, a renewal of vows with Laura at the Wee Kirk o' the Heather in Las Vegas, Prada boots, costing half a week's pay, or a (very brief) cruise to the West Indies.

He thought, by using a ruse, he might question his mother-in-law, Miranda, inventing some twaddle about checking Laura's sizes (men being universally forgiven, even coddled, for ignorance in such matters). But he could not frame a question that would elicit

the date from Laura's cool and sharp-eyed mother. She was a busy realtor, a woman of few words except where they concerned post-and-beam construction or Carrara marble in the master bath. She would not burble forth, "And that was the last time Helen and David went anywhere together as husband and wife . . ." or "I'd just bought that silver Volvo . . ." or "Do you remember how adorable Laurie's sister Angela looked; she was only a junior . . ."—remarks that could be checked against a family timeline.

Their wedding album had been no help.

It was inscribed with their names, the month and day—but, at Laura's behest, not the year. For the same reason, the photos all were in black-and-white. "Color makes pictures look dated. I want this to be always new," she'd said.

They were married December 23, and all the women, including Laura, wore red velvet, the men gray morning clothes, with top hats—even without the help of color film, he could remember the splash they all made, like bright cardinals and sparrows against the snow. The photographer spread huge sheets of clear plastic beneath an evergreen bower for outdoor shots. Laura peeked from under the hood of a wool merino cape trimmed with rabbit fur, like a character from *Little Women.*

The photos *were* timeless; not even a single car with an identifiable grille or body shape was visible.

He might have asked his own mother outright, and she would have felt no impulse to chide him. She would have been moved by his diligence.

He had missed his mother, more or less constantly, for two years, with the persistence of a low-grade fever that spiked in spring or at moments of acute need or tenderness. Laura resembled his mother in no way; she had different habits, preferences, and talents. But his wife still somehow recalled Amy, in common sense, in pure spirit. Laura still teased him about their first date: He had confessed he might never marry at all, never find a woman the equal of his mother. Amy had died of ovarian cancer, hadn't even lived to hear Amelia, the daughter they had named for her, say her grandmother's name.

Ironically, in just two years' time, if the Amelia of

today was not talking, she was sleeping. Honoring his mother, he still sometimes called Amelia "Amy," especially when he was the one putting her into her bed.

Elliott's mother was the one who, by offhand example, had instructed him in the custom that husbands, not wives, were responsible for the construction of the wedding anniversary.

This seemed only fair.

He knew that Laura assumed a titan's share of the engineering of all the other holidays, getting up at four A.M. to wash and baste great birds—one year jollying her brother, Stephen, late, when the girls were tiny and fuddled with sleep, into appearing at the doorway to their room in red-padded plush and white rabbit fur. Even Annie, the eldest at thirteen, still remained convinced she'd once glimpsed the real Santa.

Celebrating their anniversary was often deferred until New Year's Eve—with school concerts, shopping, and the arrival of Laura's three siblings, Elliott's father, and sometimes his sister all crowding the week before the holiday. Her sisters and brother stayed with Miranda in the capacious Georgian brownstone she'd occupied alone since their father's death, when Laura was only three. But Laura insisted everyone squeeze into her and Elliott's tiny saltbox for a Christmas Eve feast of seafood and pasta. Laura made everything, from the pasta to the Buche de Noel, by hand, and her labors left her so drained, she could barely nibble at the elaborate annual brunch Miranda had had catered by the Palatial Palate on the following day. Elliott had a dozen photos of Laura, asleep on the couch at Christmas dinner. One year sometime soon, he often thought, he would protest; but he could not bear to interfere with the whispered traditions and sly confidences of the MacDermotts at Christmastime, when even the slightly chilly elder sister, Suzanne, and her precocious little boy seemed to loosen up. Laura's childlike joy in her siblings was so much what Elliott hoped his girls' relationship would someday be, he knew that it must be cherished. It was so different from the vaguely affectionate diffidence of his much younger sister, who taught drama at a vast Midwestern university.

"Oh, hello," Sarah would say, uncertainly, when he

phoned her. "What's up? What do you need?" They fumbled at small talk. She sent the girls gift cards for bookstores at their birthdays.

Sarah, his mother had often said, was like their father—resolute, a survivor, self-reliant. What does that make me? Elliott wondered at the time. Wimpy? Dependent? Kindly, his mother said, noticing. Nothing to be ashamed of in a man.

But at least, he'd had his mother's example. How had Laura's siblings grown so close? Laura said the four of them had intuited early on that they must be in league against Miranda's invisible shield, become mother and father to one another or wither.

But even out of deference to the impending gathering of the clan, he did not want to put off this one anniversary, just on the off chance he would miss The Big One So Far. In the end, two weeks before Christmas, Elliott bought Laura tickets for Cirque du Soleil, their new show *Quidam,* ending a two-week run at Suffolk Downs in Boston center. Laura had been a gymnast, fighting her way on vault all the way to regionals through high school, when finally and to her sorrow, she had grown to her full height. She and their middle daughter, Rory, who took gymnastics at the local YMCA, watched tapes of the fabulous previous Cirque shows. *Allegria* was their first favorite.

When he handed her the tickets, along with a pen-drawn cartoon voucher of the two of them chewing a single strand of spaghetti at their favorite hideout, a Little Italy restaurant truly deserving of the name—just six tables—Laura, with her agile legs, jumped and clasped him about the waist like a monkey. It was a thrill to him, that was. He got a kick out of having such an agile wife, who could still do cartwheels and backbends in middle age.

"You rascal!" she cried. "This is what I wanted more than anything else in the world! I've been reading about the performances every day and just longing to see one. But the tickets are so expensive!"

"It's hardly Paris . . . ," Elliott joked, referring to the belated honeymoon they'd planned for the second summer (or had it been the first?) after their wedding, when he would have finished graduate school. Both school and Europe were nixed, never to be revisited,

by Laura's tremulous announcement that there'd been a hitch and they were pregnant.

"Oh, Paris," Laura said, "*Paris* is for the twentieth anniversary, when the girls are big enough to stay with Mother and take care of each other while being ignored beyond the basic necessities of life. That's six years from now! Annie'll be in college! And this is like a little bit of Paris, Ell! I'm so glad you got me this instead of some camisole that would make me look fat and just lie in the drawer forever."

Elliott breathed easier.

It was the fourteenth, after all, He would never forget again. Never.

In the tent, Laura reached out in the dark to clutch his hand as the hula hoop girl, ringed like an African goddess with circles of rainbow light, set first one, then three, then five circlets in motion about her hipless child's body, at one point extending her leg straight in a standing split, a hoop gyrating around her pointed toe. Down ceiling-high cables floated masked phantoms, their bloodred robes falling away, the revealed athletes then flexing and extending their impossibly taut bodies as if they were constructed of stuff other than human flesh, were instead structures of steel and ice, covered with human fabric.

Over her protests at intermission, Elliott bought Laura one of the shirts with the characteristic sunburst emblazoned in silver. "It'll show every bulge, Elliott," Laura protested.

"You haven't got bulges," he'd told her, patting the modest, tender lap of flesh over her belt, which had replaced her concave contours only after she'd given birth to the girls. He grinned to himself at a bright, momentary vision of the way his wife would look later, nude, or perhaps modeling only the tight-fitting T-shirt, ivory curve of thigh against pale blue sheets, gazing up at him from under her lids, the Lady Di parody she saved only for bed.

"At least it's stretchy," Laura told him, with a dubious pout. "It holds a person in." It would have suited her, capped sleeves and nipped waist, he later decided. After a time, he would move the shirt, still in its tissue, into his own underwear drawer. He would keep the raucous, wistful tape of the background music to

*Quidam* in his car until it snapped one day while he was driving Rory to school. He would weep, not bothering to palm away the tears, while Rory stared straight ahead, clutching her book bag.

As they left the stadium that night, pressed congenially thigh to thigh by the determined crowd, Elliott noticed simultaneously that it was eleven-thirty and that he was drunk, only a little, from the two beers quaffed at intermission on top of the wine shared at dinner. "Take a nap," Laura urged him. "I feel it, too; but I'm just tired. I can drive." She rummaged in her commodious bag—Amelia's detention slip, an open lipstick furred with cotton-swab litter, and nuggets of stale gum. "Damn," Laura griped, "this was Elizabeth Arden. Mother got it for me." She located her janitor's key ring, its anchor a metal charm featuring a laminated photo of Rory's triumphal, best-ever dismount from the beam. She kept searching.

"I'll get you another lipstick," Elliott, bleary, told her.

"I have to find some Tylenol. My eyes feel as though they're on fire from behind," said Laura.

"Too much resin in the wine," Elliott offered. "Gives you a head—"

"There." Laura held up a few lipsticky-red Tylenol. "They better help. It really hurts, Ell," she told him. "I think I have a migraine."

"Sit a moment," he told her. "We don't have to be home any special time."

"I don't like to leave Annie . . ."

"She's thirteen, Laura. You were baby-sitting half the neighborhood when you were thirteen. You bought a *car* with baby-sitting money, for God's sake."

"I did," she admitted, reclining her seat slightly. It was a quiet, ancient source of pride. "Okay, a minute."

Elliott awoke when Laura started the car. The parking lot at Suffolk Downs was empty, or nearly. He saw the hat-shaped blue-and-yellow tents billowing, and knots of the performers, gathered, smoking, looking eerily misplaced, their elaborately painted gold-and-black almond eyes shockingly adult atop their adolescent bodies. Laura had told him many of them were formerly Olympic gymnasts or ballet dancers gifted at flexibility rather than the leap or pirouette. She'd also told him that, in defiance of all logic, all dancers and gymnasts of merit smoked in order to try to stay slim and small.

"I feel better," his wife told him. "It's as if it's just pressure now, not so much pain . . . let's get home so I can lie down."

"I'm sorry, sweetie," he told her, as they entered the Sumner Tunnel, thick with Saturday-night hordes. He felt himself drifting with the pause and accelerate, pause and lurch, until Laura, in real panic, woke him.

"Elliott," she said, "the oil light is on!"

"S'nothing," he told her, "electrical glitch."

"The battery light is on now," Laura said sharply, sounding like her mother. "Is that nothing also?"

"No, that's shit," Elliott told her, abruptly sober and dry-mouthed, sitting up in disgust as the car softly drifted to a complete stop, and the lights dimmed, dimmed and disappeared. Laura dived to depress the triangular red emergency flashers; but they, logically, were also dead. Rolling across her, Elliott flipped the hood switch to signal distress, but the horns of cars behind them still burst into a cacophony of frustration. Elliott inched along the damp tunnel wall to peer under the hood.

What he saw signified as much to him as it would have had he been asked to perform surgery on a brain. Since he was a boy, gathered with his friends peering into their cars' entrails, he could never decipher the engine's mystery even when it was pointed out to him—alternator connection or brake cable, they were all the same to him. He could fill the window-washer tank and add oil, never quite sure he'd read the message of the dipstick as confidently as other men did. To start a car by crossing critical wires was a fantasy Elliott nurtured the way other men dreamed of playing rhythm guitar for Van Halen.

In moments, a K-9 police unit passed them, and the officer promised in passing to send a wrecker. Astoundingly, shortly thereafter, they were linked to some kind of shoving vehicle driven by a swarthy man Laura described as resembling the troll under the bridge, and shoved the quarter mile onto a verge of flat earth next to one of the elevators that ferried workers down into the Big Dig, the tunnel project that had made Boston a hell of dust and snarled traffic for what was promised to be three years and was now seven and counting. Despite cute, hopeful posters about the interesting things the excavations had turned up (prehistoric fish spines, colonial foundations), every single Bostonian except the fellow who owned the cranes was sick to the teeth of the project: Politicians had been threatened with recall, lawsuits filed, tourists headed for Cape Cod diverted to airports in Rhode Island.

Frantically, Laura phoned home and then, squinting, punched in their AAA road service and membership numbers, as Elliott inspected the brightly lit construction shaft and chatted with the young police officer whose tiresome duty was to guard the shaft overnight against prankish teenagers and curious drunks who tended to take dives or demonstrate their ability to balance on railings.

"The girls are fine," she reported wistfully. "The tow truck is about half an hour away. I think we'll freeze to death by then, don't you? I should have worn my long coat."

Elliott noticed scythes of slate-colored flesh under each of her eyes, as if she had applied her eye shadow upside down. One of her eyes was alarmingly bloodshot. She worked too hard, with her small design business, trifold brochures and the occasional state-sponsored pamphlet, never failing to booster every school activity and extracurricular interest the girls lit upon—enthusiasms new each year, fragile as the life span of mayflies. "But I'm not fine. I'm knocked out. I'm going to lie down in the back until the tow truck comes. I feel bad, Ell, I feel bad. My head feels funny, beyond pain . . ."

She worked too hard, Elliott told the young cop, whose name was, of course, Tony. His wife as well, Tony agreed with a sigh, offering Elliott an illicit Marlboro, which he accepted, the companiable and manly thing to do, though he'd quit smoking seven years before.

Tony's wife was a nurse at Mercy, on P.M.'s for five years. "We got two boys, four and two. We couldn't

make it without my mom and my sisters," Tony told Elliott, shaking his head in gratitude.

Elliott nodded, as if Miranda, or his father in far-off Boca Raton, ever had been any help to him and Laura. He thought, but would never have confided, that his father's twice-yearly visits, accompanied by Donna, the woman from his condo complex he described as "my lady friend," were tense affairs, not because of any lack of geniality on the part of Elliott Banner Senior, or even Donna, who brought extravagantly flowered bikinis for Laura and the girls; it was because Elliott could see plainly around Donna's neck his mother's wedding diamond reset in a pendant.

Now he strolled back to their minivan, expecting to find Laura asleep in her customary shrimp curl. What he saw instead shocked him. Laura was not given to dramatic displays, except in dire extremes. She *did* have a low tolerance for certain kinds of pain, often coming to him repeatedly during a given evening to show him her paper cut, as if she were one of the children. Now, she was braced with her spine arched against the rear seat, rocking, holding her temples with the flat of her hands. "Elliott," she whispered, "I have to go to the hospital. I don't think this is a migraine. Or if it is, I've never had one before."

"Triple-A will be here soon," he soothed her, more out of fear than any disbelief in her agony. "They can give us a jump, unless it's the alternator . . ." Elliott regarded Laura's stretched, strained face, which before his eyes seemed to fade, like the watercolor Santas and pumpkins the girls used to paint on the windows, draining from the glass in the rain. "You really are in a bad way, aren't you?" he asked, reaching for his wife's neck, hoping to cradle her. "Let me rub you down a little. Let me get in there and hold you."

"I need to go to the hospital now, Elliott," Laura moaned. Cringing, Elliott recalled how during Rory's breech birth, Laura roared at him that she wished he were dead. How did a woman who could do back-bends and cartwheels with the girls, and jump up from a fall on a friend's horse with a giggle instead of a limp, be so undone by a headache? That was Laura, though, contradictions all over the map, fitting sweetly into an amiable, slightly off-center jigsaw.

"Wait a few minutes and see," he suggested, "and then I promise I'll call for an ambulance." If he could, in fact, he would have run with Laura in his arms to the hospital. He would later realize he'd been too frightened to act, too leery of making this very real thing more so. Or had he only been embarrassed? he cursed himself.

"Officer!" Laura then screamed, and Elliott, unprepared, jumped and nearly shed a layer of skin. "Officer!"

Tony came trotting, his cigarette dangling from one corner of his lower lip. "My husband won't let me go to the hospital and I'm sick, I'm very sick!"

"I'm . . . I just said . . . ," Elliot stammered. "Laura! I'll get you to the hospital!"

"What's wrong with her?" Tony asked. Elliott shrugged helplessly.

"What's wrong with you, miss?" Laura rocked faster, faster, then suddenly stopped, dropping both hands limp at her sides.

"It stopped," she said. "My headache."

"See?" Elliott told her, baffled, trying to sound assured.

"But something is wrong, Elliott! Something is still wrong! There's a rushing in my head! I don't want to sit in this dirty hole anymore! I want to go to the hospital, where it's bright and clean . . ."

"The tow truck will be here any minute . . ."

"I need an ambulance! Elliott, now! Do you *hear* me?" She turned to Tony. "Can you cuff him? Or shoot him?" Laura asked. "I have to go to the hospital!" Tony's eyes widened, and he whirled and quick-stepped back to his radio.

"She's ordinarily a very docile person," Elliott said, as he trotted after Tony.

"Sure, I have no doubt. Who knows about this stuff? I could drive her," Tony told him, "but it's my ass if I leave here. I'm going to radio for an ambulance. Mercy is only six, eight blocks . . ."

"That's probably the best idea," he agreed. "She's way over the top. This isn't Laura. She may have food poisoning or something."

"Nothing they can do for that." Tony shrugged, cupping his lighter. "Except wait. It's gotta work itself out of her system."

"Still," Elliott persisted.

With Laura whimpering against his chest for what seemed interminable moments, her shoulders shrunken in a queerly boneless huddle, he finally heard the dim whoop of the ambulance, distant, then closer; then Tony went rushing to block the tunnel traffic with sawhorses as the vehicle backed onto the construction site. Elliott watched as Laura's hand was repeatedly jabbed for a saline IV—Laura's veins were tiny, buried, and tended to roll away. She had fainted on occasion during the most routine blood draw. When, now, she did not react nor even grimace, Elliott's stomach roiled with dazzling concern. Something *was* wrong, very wrong. The paramedics pressed ice packs to Laura's head, as waiting firefighters who had rumbled up in full gear, for no reason Elliott could discern, looked on. The smallest of the team, a woman no taller than Elliott's seventh-grader, asked if he would like to ride with his wife or follow in their car. "It's inoperative," Elliott told her. "That's how this all started."

"She struck her head?" the tiny paramedic asked, motioning for an immobilizing collar.

"No, nothing like that," Elliott told her. "The car just stopped in the tunnel, and it wasn't until we were here, waiting to be towed, that she felt the pain. No, that's wrong, it was back at Suffolk, in the parking lot."

"Was she in a lot of pain?"

"She thought she was having a migraine headache . . ."

"Does she often have them?"

"No, never. That's why she thought she must be having one," Elliott explained. "It hurt too badly for an ordinary headache."

"Have you or your wife traveled in any foreign countries recently?"

"Not unless you count Lynn," Elliott joked weakly, of the grubby neighborhood where he managed a paperback book warehouse that stocked discount chains.

"The doctor in the ER was speculating on the radio about the possibility of a virus," the paramedic said, with no trace of a smile. "Will you be coming with us, then?"

"I've ruined it," Laura whispered faintly, as he settled on a hard bench beside her and the ambulance began its impossibly rattling, jolting progress—this, Elliot thought, is how they move the frail and dangerously sick?—through the three A.M. streets. "I've ruined our anniversary. I didn't even give you your present."

"Just feel better." Elliott patted his wife's hand, noticing the odd, liverish cast of her fingernail beds. "That's the best present you could give me."

"It's in the nightstand on my side, in a silver box," Laura told him; she seemed unable to control a sagging at one side of her mouth. "There's a card. Will you look for it?"

"We'll do it tomorrow," Elliott said, as Laura was swept out of the ambulance and into the phalanx of white trousers and blue shirts.

"Wait here," a pleasant older woman instructed Elliott, "while I make a copy of your insurance card. Then we'll take you back to see what's going on with your wife." Shamed and elated that Laura had been diverted past the noisy, filthy turbulence of the waiting room (like a photo from a Third World country, head wounds seeping through gauze, mothers whose infants lie crouping, translucent green glazing their mouths and noses) Elliott scribbled what he knew of his wife's health history, splendid except for hay fever, and followed the bustling woman through automated steel doors.

In a room deliberately darkened, a physician was peering into Laura's eyes, instructing her to look up, left, right, right again. "And the pain, it started when?" he asked.

"Dinner," Laura said. "At dinner."

"You didn't tell me that!" Elliott interrupted.

"I thought it was only a headache," Laura pleaded.

"Do you have an aura?" the doctor asked, as Laura made a motion of incomprehension, as if whisking away a fly. "Did you see lightning flashes or spots at the corners of your vision?"

Laura said, "No. Just a pain that kept tightening and tightening . . . I can't explain what I mean by that . . . until it was unbearable . . ."

"I want to check something, with someone, Missus Banner," the doctor told Laura, and noticing Elliott, he said, "Hi. I'll be right back." The young doctor returned more quickly than Elliott had ever seen anyone arrive in a hospital—including during Annie's near-death joust with encephalitis—a senior colleague in tow.

The older man was perhaps just ten years Elliott's senior, but his luxuriant hair was completely white. From his bearing alone, even before he spoke, Elliott could tell that English was not his first language.

"I am Doctor Campanile, and I think we need to take some pictures of this head of yours," he told Laura, with amiable and absolute tenderness.

"Bell tower," Laura whispered.

"Do you speak Italian?"

"My choir went to Florence in high school. Florence for two days, and Paris for three days."

"Firenze." The doctor smiled approvingly, nodding as a nurse swabbed Laura's neck with a numbing solution, then inserted a white probe that appeared to have the circumference of a meat thermometer. "My parents lived in Siena. I have not seen Florence since eighty-seven."

"I went before then, in seventy-seven," Laura told him, as the doctor murmured instructions to gently move Laura onto a rolling bed at the count of three.

Elliott sat on the floor outside the imaging lab as Laura was moved slowly through the cavernous space capsule of the scanner. Since the use of his cell phone was forbidden on the corridor, he roused himself finally and found an unoccupied office with a telephone. He called AAA and learned that his car had been delivered to the dealership three blocks from his house. He glanced at his watch. It was nearly four A.M. Reluctantly, he dialed the home of his mother-in-law, Miranda, who answered on the first ring, as if she had been waiting for his call. "I'm sorry to bother you," he said, "but the girls may need you. Laura has taken ill; we're at Mercy Hospital, and Annie is alone with Rory and Amelia . . ."

"I'll go, of course," Miranda replied, "but what is the matter with Laurie?"

"She has a terrible pain in her head . . ."

"In her neck?" They both fell silent, the recollected threat of Annie's meningitis unmentionable between them.

"No, her head. And pressure. They're doing a CT scan . . ."

"Really!" Miranda said. "Should I simply bring the girls there?"

"Not yet," Elliott said. "Don't wake them. Use the key behind the light. Just wait for me to call you. I appreciate this, Miranda."

"Don't think of it," she said seriously. "You've never asked me to help with anything. I've felt quite privileged." What an odd way to put it, Elliott reflected.

He wandered back to the scanning lab, but Laura was gone, as was the doctor with the musical name. He saw the younger physician, a resident or an intern, leaning against a cabinet, filling out a form on a clipboard. "My wife," he said.

The young man smiled at Elliott, a dog's grin, slant and cringing. "You can talk to Doctor Campanile"—he pointed with his pen—"she's upstairs on the medical floor, 202, bed B. They've admitted her."

"For more tests?" Elliott asked.

"They've admitted her to the hospital," said the intern.

"For overnight?"

The younger man seemed to consider this. Finally, he said, "Yes."

Elliott jogged up the two flights and easily found Laura, propped high on pillows, dressed only in her white peasant blouse and satin undies. Dr. Campanile, as if he had been waiting in the wings for his entrance, instantly appeared at his elbow. In the other bed, an ancient, toothless crone with yellow matted hair moaned ceaselessly, "Come here, baby. Come here, baby. Come here."

"I know," Dr. Campanile told Elliott softly. "We will move her the moment we can. They are readying a private room next door." He took Elliott's arm, then gingerly, as if waiting for permission, placed his hand on Elliott's shoulder and led him to an adjacent room, where four chairs faced a low, scarred table. Three hands of poker lay abandoned on the table. Above a battered vinyl couch, a single string of white twinkle lights was strung around a stitchery sampler that read "Peace on Earth."

"The poor soul," Elliott said.

"She has no children but in her mind," Dr. Campanile told him. "They are all dead."

"Imagine, your child dying before you do."

"Yes, it is very bad. Does your wife have a family?"

"Two sisters and a brother, and her mother."

"Close by?"

"Her brother lives in Cambridge and her mother in Natick. Her sisters live, one in California, one in Chicago. She's in medical school, Angela, the one in Chicago. She was a science teacher, but she decided one year she'd always wanted to practice medicine . . ."

"You should call them."

"Why?" Elliott asked, stifling the little boy's frightened pipe in his voice. "Does my wife have a brain tumor?"

"No," said Dr. Campanile, without amplification.

"Is she very ill?"

"She will be spared a long illness," he said, "but yes, she is very ill. Let me explain what I have seen in these pictures." Deep in Laura's brain, a weakened vein, widened like a dammed estuary, present probably since her birth, had burst. "This is why she feels no pain now," the doctor continued. "It is already hemorrhaging. The pressure is gone, so there is a relief."

"But when did it burst?"

"We think perhaps in the car, some time ago."

"In the car? While we were pulled over? Why didn't I get her here sooner? What now? Will you operate?"

The doctor paused, examined his clean, clean hands, and looked up at Elliott with an anguishing discernment more expressive than words.

"Are you saying," Elliott persisted, "that Laura will be brain damaged? How bad will this be? Will she be able to function? Speak?" Read? Smile at him? Care for the children? he thought. How would they manage?

"No," Dr. Campanile replied, "she will not be brain damaged. This also she is spared. She is a strong and beautiful woman. We cannot operate, because there is nothing left for us to operate on. Nothing to remove or to clamp. There are smaller vessels in the brain, less important vessels, if you will, that can be clamped if the aneurysm is discovered in time, or the bleed caught on a scan with minimal damage. But this is a major vessel, and it is long since hemorrhaged. That is the tragedy. We could not have known it was there . . ."

"I should have known!"

"No, Mister Banner, you could not have known. She herself could not have known. She would not have had symptoms."

"Now what?"

"Now, how can I say this? It is too late. She will die, and I am sorry beyond an ability to tell you. Often, and I say often, though this condition is very rare altogether . . . this, this bubble, which is so thin, will break when the woman is in labor, so in this you are lucky, you have your children . . . and she has lived with her children and loved them. She has told me you have three girls, one large, one middle, one very small."

"Wait!" Elliott cried. "She'll die?"

"Yes."

"How long? How long does she have? How many months? Weeks?"

"Mister Banner, Elliott, it is not a case of that. I will explain to you exactly how this will happen. In several hours, or perhaps one hour, your wife will have a seizure. She will feel no pain. If she chooses, we can sedate her so that she has no awareness at all of this. She has said she does not wish us to do this."

"You *told* her?"

"She asked me. I would not lie to an intelligent person."

"You *told* her this, without me?"

"She has said she knew she was dying."

"My God! My God!" Elliott began keening. The doctor rose and gently closed the door.

"Mister Banner, let me tell you the rest of this, and then I will answer all of your questions. In one hour, or several, your wife will have a seizure, perhaps very small. She will have another, several hours later, in the morning. She may have one more, and then she will sleep; she will fall into a coma, and die this way."

"There must be something you can do."

"There is not. But, when I leave you, I will go on the Internet . . ."

"The Internet?"

"I will go on the Internet and ask all my colleagues I can find whether there is any experiment, any hope or practice . . ."

"It's the middle of the night!"

"Not in England, Australia, Germany . . ."

"But if you say there is nothing we can do . . ."

"If there is, I will find it. There are changes daily. Whatever is being tried, we will find. But I think there is nothing that can be done, except this. You can spend these hours with your wife and children, and if you wish, her family, and you can learn what she wishes. Do you have a living will?"

Angrily, Elliott told him, "Of course."

"This is a Catholic hospital. I am a Catholic. The practice, barbaric, would have been years before, to place her on life supports . . . we will do that now only if Laura chose to donate her eyes and her heart . . ."

"Her eyes and her heart?" These are mine, Elliott cried silently. His whole head was a single, black shout. "How long are we looking at?"

"Eight hours. Twelve. We cannot say."

"Twelve hours from now! But my wife was a healthy woman. She lifted weights! She did cartwheels!"

"She has lived a long time, forty years? With this in her, like, you might say, a time bomb . . ."

"How will I tell my children?" Elliott asked.

"We have a social worker who is on her way here. To stand by. And I will tell them, if you need my help. I also have two daughters. And two granddaughters." The doctor placed his hand over Elliott's. "Are you a religious man? Is Laura religious?"

"I . . . was raised a Catholic. Laura takes the children to church when they'll get up on Sunday morning. They've had their First Communions, the older ones. Laura calls herself a practicing Catholic, practicing to get it right," said Elliott, and astonishing himself, he laughed. "I suppose I'm an atheist. Or an agnostic. Too cowardly to be an atheist."

"Your wife has asked to see a priest, later. Father Conley is on his way. He can wait until she is ready."

"How . . . is Laura?"

"Well, she is not afraid. I have told her there will be no pain. That was what she feared. And she has said she is . . . she has said, like the old woman, 'My babies, my babies.' "

Now Elliott began crying in earnest.

"It is comforting, sometimes, to give up our doubts at such occasions," said Dr. Campanile, reaching out a hand, barely grazing Elliott's shoulder. "I must do it. Otherwise, I think I could not survive my work and ever eat or drink a glass of wine. We may hope, perhaps, as Our Lady instructs, for a peaceful death. Peace is not to be snored at."

"Sneezed at," Elliott corrected him, with a concealed sniff.

"I make these idiomatic mistakes all day." The doctor smiled. "Thank you."

"I'm sorry. I'm distraught. I'm . . ."

"Of course." Dr. Campanile brushed away the apology. "Are you ready to see Laura?"

Together, they walked, Elliott shuffling, conscious of his vast weariness; he might sleep for twelve hours or never again, turning into a room a door away from the sobbing old lady, whom a nurse was telling, "Soon, they will be here . . ."

"Hi, honey," Laura said, "I've really done it up now, huh?"

"Can she understand?" Elliott asked the doctor.

"Yes, I can, Ell," Laura said. "I can think as clearly as I ever could. Not that that was ever so much."

"I'll leave you alone," the doctor interrupted. "As I said, I would like to use the computer . . ."

"He's going to try to find something to help," Elliott said. "Some experimental process, somewhere in the world . . ."

"Oh, that would be wonderful," Laura said. "But realistically, he's not going to."

"How can you be so calm?" Elliott cried, dropping to his knees and grasping her hand, which smelled faintly of popcorn and her cedary cologne. "I can't bear this. Laura, I love you. I need you. There's never been anyone else for me."

"You'll be all alone." Laura reached for his cheek.

"I'll be all alone? That doesn't matter. I'll be without *you*, Laura. You, which is actually the best of me. I can't even comprehend it. I thought we would grow old together. We didn't smoke. We didn't do drugs. We ate cauliflower and drank red wine. Laura . . . your energy. You never stop, Laura. How can this be happening?

How can you stand it? Are you terrified? I shouldn't even ask that. I'm an idiot. Laura, I just want to take you in my arms and run and run until we run away from this. How can you be even sane? Sweetheart, I can't take this in! Is it true? I'm losing you . . . it's impossible for me to think past this, this black wall. I'd be jibbering like a psycho. I wouldn't be sitting there smiling."

"Why, I don't know what else to do," Laura said, the moue of her full lips suffused with pity. "I had this moment of horrid, bitter fear. I wanted to scream and hit and scratch. Then, I thought it would be easier for me than for all of you. I knew what he was going to say, Elliott. That's why I insisted so hard at the Big Dig. I thought it over. One good thing is, I won't know. I've been watching the sky, spitting snow on and off, and wondering how Mother will get here, driving five miles an hour the way she does if it drizzles. I've been watching the snow and thinking that this is the last time I will ever see snow. I'm glad it's now, Ell. Not in summer. I've been thinking that the girls would be miserable, with their birthdays in summer . . . though Christmas will always be a problem."

A problem, Elliott thought. A *problem?*

"Ell?" Laura roused him. He had fallen asleep with his head on her blanket. "It's okay. I know you're exhausted. I would sleep myself if I dared . . . miss anything. I'm so tired. But my head. You know, Ell, it feels wonderful. Just having that pain vanish. Free. I want you to do something for me."

"The donation forms."

"Oh, I did that. While you were talking to the doctor."

"You did? You didn't ask me?"

"Did you want my liver?" Laura smiled, peeking up at him like a pixie and ruffling her short blond fringe.

"No, I simply, I just thought we would discuss it."

"Ell, there's no reason for anything . . . in here to go to waste. They can even use a person's ovaries . . ."

"Laura! I can't think of that."

"Well, don't then. Because that isn't what I want you to do. I want you to go to the CVS . . ."

"Laura!" Elliott cried. "We're in a class A trauma center. What could you possibly need from the CVS drugstore?"

"Cards," Laura said. "I want you to get three wedding cards for the girls, and three graduation cards, and three blank cards, and a graduation card for my sister Angie. And a pen, a nice color. Maybe purple. And sticky notes. Can you remember that?"

"Yes, but . . . what if they don't get married?"

"Ell, most people get married."

"What if they find it grotesque?"

"They won't. It will be a shock. But they'll find it comforting. You could get a tape recorder, too, and some tapes; but I think *that* would really be more grotesque, their mother's voice . . . beyond the grave." Laura's smile was watery. "I don't really think that. I'm lying because I know I'd foul up whatever I had to say, or bawl, and that would break their hearts. Can you give me my makeup kit?"

"What about me?"

"I've left you a card. Remember? In the nightstand at home."

"What about me? Forever?"

"Well, I'm sorry it has to be you, my love, my dear love, but you'll be good at this, Elliott. You're a very practical person. You make conscious choices. You think everything over. *Everything.* And we'll make notes. Before . . . anything happens. Before I call Mother to bring the girls. I don't want her to wake them now."

"Are you sure you want me to leave you now and go to the CVS?"

"It's only a block away. It's open twenty-four hours, I'm sure."

"I mean, leave you?"

"They said it will be hours, or an hour at least . . . before . . . and then I'll be . . . pretty okay until the next one. The doctor said."

"I don't want to leave you," Elliott told her, burying his face in her lap, smelling her skin. He felt a part of himself, below his heart, above his waist, give way like a broken button. That was what they mean, he thought, when they say *a part of me died.* An organ lapsed into repose, disuse, murdered by disbelief.

"Well, we don't have all that much time. Please, Ell. And get me my makeup kit. From my purse. I want to clean up."

"Can you get out of bed?"

"I can do anything I want," Laura said. "I'm dying."

She washed her face carefully with the coarse bar soap provided in the hospital's tiny steel cubicle of a washroom. She hated to use soap on her face. It was a source of pride to her that she had no crow's-feet and skin as soft as Rory's. But this was of no consequence now. On impulse, she then decided to shower and wash her hair. She rang for a nurse, who, eyes wide with shock, helped her negotiate the IV pole, use a plastic packet of shampoo (Laura refused the offer of conditioner), and slip into a flowered gown, snapped in back. While she was towel-drying her hair, the same nurse reappeared with an embroidered bed jacket, evergreens and snowmen.

"Did this belong to a person who died?" Laura asked kindly. "Not that I would mind."

"No, it was a gift for one of the nurses," the young woman told Laura. "She wants you to have it. She's having bunion surgery and will have to spend a month in bed. We all chipped in. But she would rather you have it."

"Well, no, I shouldn't take it. But, okay, please thank her," Laura said. "It sure is pretty. My daughters will like me to be pretty."

"We . . . don't . . . we're so sorry," said the young nurse, who looked no older than Ellliott's sister, Sarah, perhaps twenty-five.

"I know. It's terrible. And at Christmas, too. I feel bad for *you.*"

"We'll try to help in every way, Missus . . ."

"Laura."

"Laura, okay, do you need anything?"

"Ummm, I'd love a cup of coffee. I have to think," Laura said, more to give the nurse a mission than from any desire. Coffee, she thought. If there is life after death, I will miss coffee. And Italian lemonade. My signature, so practiced on my college spiral notebooks, Laura MacDermott Banner. Also, ironing. Laura loved the plain usefulness, the simple gratification of making a wrinkled thing fresh and crisp. I will miss swimming in the cold Atlantic. Asparagus. Rory's hair when she comes out sweating after her workout. Auburn spikes, like a punk rocker.

Rory was tough as nails.

At eight, Rory was almost finished, but still young enough to heal without a grudge against the world.

Annie, well, Annie would be angry, for ever so long. At thirteen, she had the duty to be angry no matter what, even if events offered her no insult. She would need serious help. She would give Elliott a hard ride, particularly if he ever remarried. Little Amelia. Amelia, born of Elliott's grief at the prospect of losing his mother, Amy, a woman more dear to Laura than her own mother—the real Grandma, who came to stay for weekends and shooed them out to dinner and movies, who cleaned the blinds and made Laura take naps while she was nursing the new baby—Amelia was not yet three.

She would fare best of all. *Particularly* if Ell remarried.

Laura had no memory of her own father.

Laura looked at the telephone. The doctor, so handsome and dear, like an archangel, had told her to call anyone she wanted, anywhere, on the house. She would call her sisters soon, before Elliott returned. She pictured him puzzling over cards, searching racks for the right thing, frazzled and distracted, raking at his dark hair.

Should she call the boy who framed the pictures of the girls Laura saved from their plays and sporting events, taking lavish care, with innovative mattes and artful woods? Who had once asked Laura to come to see his own pictures, to meet him at his loft in darkest Lynn, not far from Ell's warehouse? And she had gone, and he had sketched her, lying on his red futon after she had allowed him to undress her and fondle her to an aching crisis, but not to penetrate her, giving as the excuse their lack of protection. How he had told her he loved her, how he had adored her skin, calling it bisque, old-worldly, as if never touched by sun. And Laura had thanked him, in turn, for his worshipful gentleness, kissed his hands and his chest with its single tendril of gold hair. She had accepted this afternoon as a gift for a woman just turned forty, newly spayed, just like their dog, Athena, in and out, one bright afternoon, a Band-Aid on her tummy the only testimony to her lapsed wish for the three more children they never would be able to afford. At closed confession the following week, knowing by his voice the priest was the youngest of the three, she described her immeasurable lust, which had not dissipated. And she remembered his mild voice, no surprise in it, telling her that they were human and therefore liable to sin, giving her no penance beyond her own reflections about the promises she'd made before the altar.

Should she call the boy? She had adored the heat of his muscled belly, the abrupt virility of everything about him, his nutty art-stoked passion, adored him over and over again, many nights in her mind when her sleep was restless. No, he would sometime find out. Elliott would bring photographs to the store, to be made into a tape, or a collage for the girls. He would recognize Laura in the pictures and ask after her. Laura smiled, a little abashed, at the notion of his grief.

But there was another matter.

Elliott would find the sketch. She had not been able to bring herself to burn it.

Well, thought Laura, brushing her hair, he would not find it for a long time, and it was not signed. Would it make Elliott happy or sadden him to know she was still . . . desired? Even in memory? Would he doubt her love for him, which was absolute, or understand that the picture represented a momentary lapse? In any case, there was nothing she could do about it now, and she would not know of his reaction, unless she should linger and become a ghost.

I would love to be a ghost, Laura thought.

When they were children, in Sunday school or waiting for dinner, idly playing what-if games, wishing for super powers, hers had never been for bags of gold or eternal life but always for invisibility—the gift of stealth to invade secret places, overhear adult conversations, glide up to the teacher's desk during the math exam.

What would she do with it as a permanent condition?

Eavesdrop, of course. Whenever and however she might. Pull pranks on Elliott as he sat reading *Motor Trends* on the toilet. Knock the magazine just beyond the reach of his hands while his pants were around his ankles. Wake him with a soft whisper as he slept, a breath on his cheek that smelled of her. Perhaps, see him fall in love again. She had read that the famed magician Harry Houdini, a boy from Wisconsin, had promised his wife that after his death, he would send her a sign to prove there was life beyond this life.

I would do that, Laura thought, send Elliott a message from me, telling him that I was fine, that I loved him still, and even more, that it was fine with me for him to fall in love again. I would make him trip when he tried to dance at his wedding, she thought, nearly giggling, reckoning Elliott might need no help at that. The notion of such a wedding, of her girls slightly older, in the strappy dresses they would wheedle Elliott into buying, thrust her into no state of jealousy, only a wistful smoothness of mood, as if it really were true what Saint Julian of Norwich said, that all manner of things should be well. And what if they finally all were? Would she twirl away then, like a twist of snuffed candle smoke, her earthly purpose fulfilled? Or hang around? Visiting at intervals?

Yes, Laura thought, not all ghosts would suppose their work in life unfinished, the common theory. Some might simply be . . . curious. Oh, to watch the girls develop, nudge them toward the right sizes at the lingerie counter, to float in the backseat at Annie's prom, witness that first ecstasy. To cheer, unseen but felt, at Rory's first triumph in the all-around?

To hazard a touch, perceived, perhaps, only as an arrow of sunlight, or a puff of wind, on Amelia's hand at her first day of school.

She had read—where? Somewhere—that spirit entities often manifested themselves as columns of icy air or scented breezes. Laura would not be a cold spot. She would be a breeze, a warm, perhaps even mischievous gust.

Laura tried to imagine her clingiest girl, her baby, the one who was frightened of everything from skeleton masks to pictures of snakes on television, standing proud and wide-eyed with her first backpack, after all those years of pretend homework with Laura at the kitchen table. All those lines and curlicues Laura and Amelia gravely pretended were letters and numbers

coalescing into something intelligible. Being there, a gentle tendril of air, for only her child to feel, a nudge of encouragement, like a steadying hand at her back. She tried to picture Amelia age-progressed, missing a front tooth.

Once she had allowed herself to go this far, she could not blinker her mind's eye. The weddings. Annie, sliver-thin and severe in a sheath with not a single furbelow. Rory . . . dancing every dance. The births of the girls' children . . . now, Laura instructed herself firmly, that is enough. She put her hands flat on the mirror and pushed. She could not tolerate hurtling forward, to a time when they . . . would not remember her, except as an idea that would prompt a tear, perhaps if they played "Mom's" favorite song. She had applied new concealer, and eye shadow, which she would not weep into stains.

Crossing to the telephone, she called her mother and asked her to wake the girls. Miranda already had, and said she was just leaving the house, in any case.

Laura then dialed her little sister, Angela. Angela was a slow waker, a source of concern to her as a third-year medical student. It took copious coffee and time to get her to a state of full alert.

So Laura was not surprised when Angela did not recognize her voice at first. "Doctor MacDermott," Angela said. "Doctor MacDermott here."

"It's Laurie, Angie. Do you hear me?"

"It's Doctor MacDermott."

"Can I talk to Cobb, Angie?" Laura heard the phone's muffled fall, and Cobb's voice rising into a question as he took it up. Cobb was a surgical resident. Was Miranda sick? Or one of the girls?

"No, it's me," Laura said. "I'm in the hospital and you have to explain to Angie that . . . actually, I'm dying." Shame was her transitory sensation. It was so bald, so melodramatic.

"Laurie, wait. This doesn't make sense."

"I know. But it's true."

"Laurie!" Cobb was that rare human, a physician with an almost comic absence of arrogance. This was what Angela, who had sworn not to become involved until she was finished with all her studies, had been unable to resist. He loved them all, like a fifth MacDermott sibling.

"I haven't got much time," Laura said. "So, Cobb, listen."

"I am," he told her seriously. Cobb was solid.

"I don't know if this thing—Elliott will explain it—is hereditary. My father died young. He had a stroke. She has to have her blood pressure monitored and have her head examined." Laura realized what she had said and tried to stifle a snort of laughter. "I mean, her brain scanned. For an aneurysm."

"I promise, Laurie," Cobb said. "Can I put Angie on now?"

"Laurie?" Angie's voice was still thick with sleep. "What's wrong?"

"Angela, I'm so proud of you," Laura said. "And you know I love you best of all." She could hear Cobb's voice murmuring behind her sister's.

"What? Why?" Angela began to hiccough, then wail, "Where are you? Mercy? Let me talk to the doctor."

"He's out looking for help, writing e-mails to doctors

all over the world, he is," Laura said. "If there's a way to help, he'll find it. He's very good. But you can't get here to talk to me in person by the time this is over."

"I have to see you! There has to be a flight!"

"It's snowing. You know they'll close the airport."

"I'll get there!"

"I want you to come for Christmas, whenever it's safe to travel, and be with the girls and Elliott. And I want to tell you I love you best. I was like a mother to you, and you were my little dressup doll . . . I know this sounds schmaltzy, Angie, but I have to tell you, it's what you think at a time like this. Your life really does go on instant replay."

"Laurie! Don't! Laurie, you loved Stephen best!" She listened as Angela covered the phone and yelled to Cobb, "Get the airline on the cell phone! Get a flight for us! Now, right now!" And then she came back on. "Is Stephen there?"

"No, not yet. But I want you to remember. Stephen was our big older brother. He was the chief torturer, the big cheese, the big tease. I loved him"—Laurie

thought, *I am using the past tense*—"best next to you. He was a *guy*. We all had to take care of him. And he had to take care of us. He was the daddy. And Suzie just wanted to grow up and get out of the house. That left us."

"Is Elliott there?" her sister asked.

"He's at the drugstore," Laura explained. "I wanted him to get me some things."

"At the *drugstore*?" Angela brayed.

"Yes, I don't have time to explain. Before I hang up, I want to tell you, Suzanne had Mother. You had me. There are things you will always remember about me. Remember when I painted you as a Picasso for Halloween? All blue on one side and all yellow on the other? Remember when I read you *Little House in the Big Woods*, and you wanted to move to Wisconsin and live in a log cabin, and we got the plans from the library . . ."

"And stole the lumber. Stephen could have been a full-time thief . . . ," Angela, now fully awake, said roughly.

"He built the tree house! He could have been a builder or an architect!"

"If he wasn't a full-time screw-off . . ."

"Don't say that, Angie," Laura reproved. "Stephen's just . . . it's a phase . . ."

"He's forty-two, Laurie!" Angela snorted, and there *was* no arguing it: Stephen, the man for whom the term "peripatetic" had been invented. He was a sometime laborer, a sometime roadie for bands, a sometime collector of seasonal unemployment.

"Think of how he built you that house, so you could pull up the rope and no one could get you? But then you really did it? And we threatened to call the fire department? You didn't care, and we actually had to call them? You were so gutsy, Angie. What were you, five?"

"How can you do this?"

"I know it hurts. It hurts me to remember, too. But I have to do it all right now."

"I mean, leave me, and then talk to me as if it were any other day."

"I don't have any choice. I told you that! Ell and I

went to Cirque du Soleil for our anniversary, and it was so wonderful, and then I got this massive, this incredible pain in my head . . ."

"Don't you dare leave me before I get there."

"I'll try hard," Laura said, relenting, wondering how a brain could will itself not to wink out.

"Laurie, I love you! I love you! I'll, when I graduate, I'll find a way to stop this . . ."

"No, you take care of babies, the way you want to."

"Laurie!"

"I have to call Suzie and Stephen. Well, Stephen will probably come over. So I have to hang up." The voice that replied was Cobb's.

"I think she's . . . throwing up, Laurie. I'll watch over her. I have a plane flight. We'll be there by . . . I think by noon. They're still landing. I want to tell you, I wish you could be at our wedding," he said. "I'm sorry I said that."

"Some would say I *will* be, huh?" Laura answered.

"We'll have a picture . . ."

"Oh, Cobb, no, ick!" Laura answered, as Elliott, wet and disheveled, entered the room with a double hand-

ful of plastic bags. "That would be so morbid. It will be summer then. A long time from now."

She thought of her mother-in-law's garden, as it was when Amy was alive, the riots of bleeding heart, gerbera daisies, hosta like great umbrellas spoked by the stargazer lilies. Laura was a disaster with her own garden. She was limited by inclination and sheer languor—weeds and worms? Or books and oatmeal cookies?—to hydrangea and *Rosa rugosa.* Elliott called Laura the Black Thumb, after she was able to pull off the impossible and murder a cactus dish garden. "Kiss Angela," she told Cobb, and put the phone down, turning her attention to her husband, getting up off the bed. Why should she be in bed? Had anyone told her to stay in bed, or did people simply compliantly slip onto these hard beds with their stiff, many-times-darned sheets the moment they were designated "patient"?

"Did you find the things?" she asked her husband, reaching out with the towel from the end of her bed to dry the sleet from his drooping black curls.

"Yes, all of them," Elliott said, and just then Laura

dropped the towel and groped back, her arms rowing, as if for an imaginary chair. Her eyes revolved away until only a slim sliver of the blue iris showed, and her hands clawed as if she were attempting to grasp her own wrists. Elliott dropped the bags and shouted for the nurses, who came in a group of three. They all watched as Laura's feet slowly attained a perfect level en pointe.

"Don't worry, Mister Banner," the young one said. "She won't bite her tongue. She doesn't feel this."

Laura's jaws were scissoring, her teeth grinding louder than a cement mixer in the silence of the predawn. "It will end in a moment. I'll get Doctor Campanile."

He stroked Laura's sweaty forehead and smoothed back her clean hair. "You smell good," Dr. Campanile told Laura. "Do you feel odd?"

"Only tired, as if I'd gone running."

"Sleepy?"

"No."

"That's good, too."

"You didn't see it," Elliott pleaded. "It must have hurt her terribly."

"I know patients who have grand mal seizures chronically, and they say there is no pain," the doctor told him. "They feel as if they are far away from their own bodies. They can hear, however." He spoke softly, then, "Well, I think it is time to call your daughters now. She is fine, for a good while perhaps."

"They're on their way. Will they see this? When it happens again? There was no warning."

"No. I hope not. I can't say for certain. We will let them wait outside. I'll be right outside. Every moment. The office I am in is only three doors from the nurses' station. I'm still searching, Mister Banner. I'm speaking online with a neurosurgeon in Australia. He's had some success with preserving a life, but not with much brain function . . ."

"That would be all right," Elliott told the doctor. "I would care for her."

"It would *not* be all right, Ell," Laura said. "I don't want that."

"Laura, let him check it out, at least. For me."

She sighed. Elliott left to find a glass of water.

"Doctor," Laura said, as he fiddled with the lines in her IV, summoned a nurse to inject something, "only for relaxation," he promised. "Am I forgetting something?"

He paused thoughtfully. "I have seen so many deaths, so many rooms in this place ringing with anguish for unfinished lives. I have watched children die. In my experience, the worst deaths are the deaths of those who have failed to love their lives."

"I do love my life," Laura said. "It is a small life, though."

"But a complete life. I don't mean completed, but lived. So, for you, I suspect it is less difficult. There is less to hope to have accomplished. I hope to be as strong," the doctor said.

"But you don't really have an alternative, do you?" Laura asked him. "When there is nothing left but this, you don't think of yourself. It isn't bravery. It's something else."

"This is the same thing I observe," said Dr. Campanile. "It is something else. Perhaps emotional, perhaps biology being our comfort and friend. Now rest, Laura, save your strength."

Laura brushed her hair again and made the call to her sister Suzanne. Suzanne gave a short, sharp scream. She then insisted there must be a second opinion; she would call her best friend's husband, a professor at UCLA, who would know what to do, perhaps the Mayo Clinic. A Medevac. Laura demurred. Suzanne was adamant. She would call back and ask to speak directly to the neurologist. Suzanne was an administrator for a large credit union. She coped by taking charge. Laura said nothing. Suzanne then resolutely, over Laura's objections, roused Laura's ten-year-old nephew, Aaron, who told Laura he had done his project on Paris and pasted in the photos she had sent him of the churches. At Suzie's prompting, he sang one line of the French carol he had learned.

This, more than anything, nearly did Laura in.

At last, Suzanne took the phone back from Aaron.

"Well," she said gruffly, with a pause that let Laura know she'd lit a cigarette (Suzanne believed that none of them knew she smoked), "you are the best of us, the

most beautiful, the most patient, the kindest . . ."

"Suzie, you are far more attractive than I ever was. Men *fought* to date you. I only ever had Elliott, and Greg in high school," Laura said. At forty-six, divorced for nine years, Suzie was still stunning, slender as a champagne flute, ankles like a thoroughbred. "And what have I done with my life? A couple of pamphlets for county fairs and motorcycle rallies? Made Halloween costumes?"

"You've . . . lived an honest life. I'm Mother, of course. I know you all think that. Cold and remote. But Laura, don't think . . . don't think . . ." She detected no wobble in her sister's voice, but Laura knew Suzanne was crying. "Stephen will be absolutely lost," Suzie said, her own analysis of their chronically single, helplessly charming brother, who often said he wished he were gay so he could find someone as neurotic as himself. "And Angela . . ."

"She has Cobb. So you'll come, then?"

"Of course, I was already coming today. Our flight is in three hours. Do you think . . . ? That we . . . ?"

"I don't know. It could be. But Suzie, listen. I have

to ask you . . . there is one thing that I want you to do. You know my desk? My little desk in the bedroom, not the computer room?"

"Grandma MacDermott's."

"Well, I want you to have that, because I know you love it, but Grandma thought I was going to be a writer, a real writer, I mean, that was why she left it to me . . ."

"You wrote all those poems . . . when we were little."

"Yes, about dead dogs and virgins jumping into the volcano. I wish I could get hold of *them*, too. Mother probably has them. But what I really want is, there's a locked compartment in it. To the left of the opening for your knees. I have the key taped under the big lid. Where I keep my stationery? That you gave me?"

"What did Grandma have in there?"

"A Valentine. That's all. Not signed. I was so excited when I found it. It's so old, it has real lace."

"What do you have in there."

"That Valentine. And also a little charcoal sketch. Of me. A nude sketch. Rolled up. From . . . a long time ago. Will you take that out for me, and . . . decide what to do with it? One of the girls, when she's as old as I am now, maybe she'll want it, if one of them shows signs of wanting to draw or something. They don't show signs of that now."

"I'll do that. And if I can't, I'll destroy it."

"Okay," Laura said, a burden lifted. "Suzie? I didn't have an affair."

"It wouldn't matter, but I believe you, Laurie. Of anyone on earth, you are the last person I would suspect of having an affair." Laura didn't know whether to feel grateful or slighted. "I'm going to get Aaron and me to the airport *now*. We'll get the earliest flight. They let you bump in for things that are urgent."

There was a long pause. Then Suzanne said, "Laurie? Baby?"

"What, Suzie?" Laura asked.

Suzanne said softly, "Sleep tight." And she put down the phone without saying good-bye.

* * *

Elliott watched Laura, in her tiny, flawless, Catholic-school script, taught her by nuns who were allowed to write home only twice a year, as she filled all the space on all the cards, licked and labeled them: Anna, Aurora, Amelia. She saved Angela's graduation card for last and left it open. "Put a check in it, Ell," she told him. "A big check. She has pots of loans to pay off. Will you do that?"

"We have three girls to educate, Laura," he reminded her, hating himself.

"But Ell, I'm so young! And you didn't want to take out insurance on me, remember? You said I was basically an at-home mom? But I said that was all the more reason, that I wasn't a real contributor so it would be like a sort of savings account for the girls? Well? You'll have piles of life insurance! You'll be rich, by our standards. You can take them to Paris, when Amelia is big enough. Will you do that, Ell? Will you?"

He promised.

He could not imagine doing anything like that.

"And I don't care," Laura added, "if you take a new

wife with you. I really want you to get married again, Elliott. I mean it. You're the marrying kind." Both of them smiled. This has been a private joke all their lives together. It had been Elliott, not Laura—Laura yearned to travel and "be free and poor"—who begged to marry early, and he was relieved when the accidental pregnancy happened. Elliott didn't want to leave home even to visit the Grand Canyon, much less the Grand Caymans, and had spent three weeks assembling a folder of tips, maps, and coupons for a five-day excursion to Disney World with a one-day stop to see his father.

Oh, Elliott, she thought. If only I could donate something from my body to you . . . something, some gene on which was encoded the will to take chances.

Laura felt the urgent need to begin to dictate her list, spraying out information like scattershot, in no order of importance: *There were stickers in the heartworm box Elliott should put on the calendar to remind him to give Athena her pills. All the doctors' and dentists' names, including the orthodontist Rory would surely need, were in the left-hand drawer of her office desk, in a file marked Girls/Personal. Baptismal records and birth certificates, with copies, were in the same folder. Their life insurance policy and their wills were in the fireproof safe. The combination was 6345789. He must ask for Miss Cook for Amelia for first grade. Rory is only paid up at the gym until February, and the Y coach said she'd gone beyond him; she needs private instruction.*

"Oh!" she cried suddenly. "I forgot all my friends!" The scope of her ability to attend had diminished to a single point of concentration, like the pinprick cameras they made with Sister Julian in fourth grade, with shoeboxes and black construction paper. She could see only her family in that small lighted circle. "I need more cards, Elliott! I need one for Rebecca and Whitney! And one for the women in the book club, Marley and Elizabeth . . ."

"I'm not getting any more cards," Elliott said, his features visibly blurred with exhaustion. "You've gone far enough with this. It's like you're organizing a fund-raiser."

Laura bit her lips. "You're right," she said. "But you will tell them, especially Rebecca and Whitney, how much I . . . ?"

"Laura, could you possibly think they don't know?"

"I would want a good-bye," Laura said, biting her lip thoughtfully. "And I can't bear calling them." At last, Laura asked a nurse for a sheet of plain paper and wrote what she actually felt, rather than what she thought she should: *Miss me, you guys. Miss me and talk about me. Try to include the girls with your kids, and help Elliott find a wife.*

"That's insulting," Elliott said. "You make it sound like, make sure the poor old doofus buttons up his sweater. I would never, ever get married again. Who could love the girls the way I do? Who could I love . . . the way I love you? It's ridiculous. Laura, don't. It's crude."

"Elliott," Laura said suddenly, "people always say they never will. And they mean it. But I've read articles that say if you like being married, chances are you'll marry again within two years. It's people who don't like being married who stay widowers."

"And furthermore, with all this, there's no time for me, for us. I want to hold you, forever. I want to tell you all the things I've thought about, when I see you making dinner, how sexy it is to me that you know where everything is, how you sing when you fold the laundry, always the same song, did you know that?"

"I didn't," Laura replied suddenly. "What is it?"

"It's 'Hey, Big Spender,'" Elliott said, nearly laughing. "That's what it is."

"Huh," Laura said, her eyes welling, as she took Elliott's arm. "It probably looks like I care about you less than I do about all these others. I know I'm wheeling from one thing to another . . . but Elliott, it's not that I love you less, I love you *more.* I guess I expect you to be another me, part of me. To understand more. I . . . I was going to ask you if you wanted to make love—it wouldn't hurt me, and it would be our last chance." Elliott winced, caught his breath. "I knew you'd react that way, sweetie. I understand. It probably would be too . . . appalling. Like making love to a—"

"No, not that! Not at all. But I . . . couldn't, Laura," Elliott told her. "I would be afraid to hurt you. What I wanted was to be alone. Hold you . . . to sleep. No more rushing around."

"And, Ell . . . we have time. But now we'll have to

wait before we talk anymore," Laura said, with a significant and patently phony brightening of her eyes as she glimpsed her daughters, huddled at the doorway, Amelia still in her Clifford pajamas. Miranda, exquisitely turned out in camel and taupe Saturday elegance, stepped into the opening behind the girls.

"She wouldn't change," Miranda apologized to Elliott, gesturing at Amelia, then leaning down to kiss his cheek. He hoped his mother-in-law did not notice how he flinched. She kissed Laura's cheek and said, "I wrestled with her for thirty minutes." How inappropriate Miranda must have felt dragging a rumpled child in pajamas into a hospital, Laura mused.

Amelia would not cross the room to her mother's bed. Annie hung back, as well. It was Rory who cried, "Mommy!" and flung herself on top of Laura.

"Don't!" Elliott cried, as Rory froze.

"It's okay, Ell," Laura told him. "She can't hurt me. It's okay, Rory, Rory, morning glory, sun queen of the balance beam. This is so terrible, if I had a million bucks, I would give it away if you didn't have to see me like this."

"You don't have a million bucks," Rory said. "You don't look sick, Mommy."

"But I am, honey," Laura said slowly. "It doesn't show. It's inside."

"Like cancer?"

"Sort of, but no." Laura sighed, thinking she was possibly the only person in the entire United States tonight who actually wished she *did* have cancer. "Hand me that sticky paper, honey, will you?" Laura asked Rory. "I don't want to forget everything." She printed, *Coat moisturizer for dog all gone. Cleaning to be picked up at Cantorini's. Save one of my rings for each of the girls— my grandmother's for Annie. Find a grief group, one for each age. Ask the woman I know, Paula Miles, at Hospice.* The impossibility of compressing an entire lifetime of routines and assumptions so instinctive they were like swallowing, not something she had to remind herself to do, was like describing the color orange to a person blind from birth. But had they been struck and killed in the tunnel, somehow all of them would have grown up. Laura's sister Angela was their legal guardian. But of course, they'd no need of a guardian.

They had a father.

She'd grown up.

She'd had a mother.

Hastily, she scribbled: *Find daycare provider IN HOME. Advertise through the college. Emphasize child-development training with children who have problems.* She could think of no other thing to add except, *Do this no matter what it costs, for a minimum two years.*

Laura finally put down her pen and asked, "Do you want me to talk to all three of you alone, without Daddy and Grandmother? Or each one at a time?"

"All together," said Rory, beckoning to Amelia, who stuck her thumb in the corner of her mouth and shook her head violently. She stuck out one of her red Clifford slippers, new since St. Nicholas Day, for Laura to see. Laura smiled and pointed.

"Well, if my vote matters at all to anyone, I would like to talk to you alone without them," said Annie, gesturing at her sisters and her father. Glancing her up and down, Laura was heartsick to see that Annie had chosen to wear a skirt and blouse and had French-braided her hair. Rehearsing for a funeral, she thought.

"Okay, well, that's okay, right?" Laura asked the room at large, noticing that the sun, in a piercingly clear sky, was on the horizon. Despite the snow, there would be stars tonight.

Elliott obediently scooped Amelia up and led Rory out. After a moment, Miranda followed.

Annie sat down across from Laura in the straight chair. There was only one, and it looked as comfortable as a barstool. "Why don't you come here and sit beside me?"

"Obvious reasons," Annie said, curling her lip.

"I don't smell or have anything catching," Laura snapped.

"I mean I would obviously cry."

"Oh."

"And that wouldn't get anything cleared up."

"Do we have to clear things up?"

"Yes, a couple," Annie said. She has made her own

list, Laura thought, blinking furiously, pretending to fluff her pillow.

"To begin with, I was the one who stole the twenty dollars; I'm sorry I called you a bitch in the letter, which was from me; and I'm going to have my period soon. I smoked a cigarette at Justine's. I bit Amelia just last night because she hit me with her lousy makeup bag and I have a huge welt on my head."

"Well, I know all those things," Laura replied, trying to keep her voice even. "Not that you bit Amelia. That's a little over the top. But it shows you're a good person that you wanted to tell me. As for your period, well, just use my things. They're under the bathroom sink. Put the pad in your underpants. I always liked the pads because they don't hurt or get stuck, even if they are messier, and don't believe anybody who says you can't swim or exercise or anything . . ."

"I meant, you *won't* be there with me! Nice!" Annie hissed.

"Do you think I picked this time to die?"

"It really sucks. How can your mother do two hundred crunches a day and then die in eight hours?"

Laura shrugged. "I'm not doing it voluntarily."

"Dad says there is a surgery."

"I'd be mental. Not just mental. I'd have to be fed with a tube. I wouldn't know who you were."

"How do you know?" Annie asked, clenching her fists with their violent purple-and-glitter tips. "How do you know what you'd know? Don't you think you kind of owe it to us to try *something* instead of just laying there in a nice Christmas jacket and dying?"

"Anna Lee," Laura said sternly, "I heard what the doctor said, and he said it would be useless. On top of that, you would come to hate me."

"I hate you for not doing it! How do you like that?"

"Not much."

"I hate you for being so selfish you don't even think of Daddy or the poor baby. She won't even remember you!" Annie screeched.

"Do you want her to remember me as a thing that had to be turned over in bed for her sores and fed through a hole in her stomach? Because that's how it would be, Annie. I'm not lying. I don't want to say

that to you, but that's how it would be. You have to help the baby remember me, Anna Lee. You have to help her."

"Thanks a lot! I suppose I have to be the big grown-up now like you did when your father died, because Dad is going to be this huge limp psycho, and I'm going to have to take care of Rory and the baby and totally have no life of my own! Thanks!"

Until now, Laura had not regarded her family history as particularly tragic. Too late, she saw it for the disjointed thing it had been. "I don't expect that! Dad will take care of you, and Grandmother . . ."

"Oh, *Grandmother*! She's *so* sweet!"

"Well, I think this will change her. It changes people," Laura said stoutly. "Anyhow, Anna Lee, don't you feel even a little sorry for *me* that I have to leave *you*? I'm the one in this dumb bed, after all. I'm the one who got stuck in the Big Dig, when I should have come here right away . . ."

"Could they have done anything if you had come sooner?" Annie's face was suddenly a child's again, as if the sun had shouldered its way from behind a threatening cumulonimbus. A child's face, helplessly broken open by hope.

"No, absolutely, honey. No, it would have made no difference at all." Laura tried to soothe her.

"You should sue the city!"

"For having a lousy old car?"

"For keeping the ambulance from getting there faster! People do it all the time. They sue for everything!"

"Anna, please . . . ," Laura pleaded. "You have every right to be angry with me, but I wish you wouldn't do this now, because you'll hate that you did it later and that will make you feel lousy . . ."

"Which brings me to another thing," Annie said. Laura wished she had a watch. She feared Annie was using up her allotted time. Everyone had to have a piece of time. There was her mother to think of, and Elliott, her siblings.

"What else?" she asked.

"I want to change my name," Annie told her. "I want to be named after you."

"Laura? I don't think Anna Laura sounds too . . . it doesn't go together."

"No, *Annie* Laurie. I happen to know that's what you wanted to name me. But *Dad* wanted to name me after that stupid song, about the cherry tree and the little old farmhouse, and you gave in, like you always do." Annie's fury was fearsome. In her ignorance, Laura had believed this reaction would take years to unveil itself.

"Well, I don't always give in, but you're right." Though practically geriatric by the standards of their crowd when they married, Elliott had insisted on naming Anna after a stupid Al Kooper song, simply because he had worn out the album playing the bass organ riff over and over. "You can change your name if you want. You don't even have to go to court. You just change it. Start by changing your school papers. I will love your being named after me."

"Because that was my baby song, you know!" Annie said, standing up, her stocky little frame a pillar of rage. "You sang it to me. For love of Anneee Lauree, I would lay me *doon and dee*!"

"You remember that, my darling, darling?"

"Yeah, I remember," Annie said, turning to stalk from the room, shouting, "Next!"

"Wait!" Laura called, sitting up. "Let me touch you, Annie. Not for you. For me." Annie, dragging her feet, crossed the floor and held out her hand. Laura kissed her still-a-child's palm and before closing Annie's fingers, whispered, "Look at your lifeline, Annie, long and strong! Gosh, you'll be an old babe! And how many lovers cross your heart line, one coming up pretty soon!" Annie's lips twitched. Oh, St. Anne, Laura prayed, help me not to break and beg. Help me be the mother you were. "Annie, you're my heart. Annie, forgive me." She looked up at her daughter, whose eyes were fixed on the rising sun. "You can send Rory now," Laura whispered, releasing Annie's hand, grateful to see she held it still gently closed. Annie stood by the bed, so erect her back was nearly arched, straight as a cadet, and stared out the window.

"The sun is coming up, finally," Annie said, "and it's not snowing so much. Probably won't have a white Christmas."

She did not look down at her mother; but neither did she move.

*   *   *

In the quiet room, where other people only wept or slept, Elliott offered his mother-in-law a cup of coffee. He peered into the pot. Even to his indifferent nose, it smelled burnt.

"I think I should make a new batch," Elliott told her, "but there doesn't seem to be any coffee or filters."

"I'd rather have tea," Miranda told him. Elliott rifled a grubby little basket. He found tea bags.

"Hot water from the tap?" he asked brightly.

"No, *Elliott.* Just take plain water and run it through the coffee machine once to clean it out, then do it again so it boils. Wouldn't *you* rather have tea also?" Miranda asked him. "It's calming." She tried to pull Amelia up onto her lap, but Amelia, who sat bobbing her thumb in her mouth and staring catatonically at two four-legged cartoon creatures—both vaguely shaped like televisions, who seemed to alternate between bashing each other with kitchenware and dancing in circles—kicked both her stout legs like pistons, until Miranda, with a nearly inaudible cluck of her tongue, let her go.

Elliott heard the tiny criticism, though, and noted it.

He found himself watching the cartoon creatures, which had now stuck themselves together with some kind of glue, butt to butt.

"I think we can pour it now," Miranda told him with a slight cough. "I am parched."

As he handed her a paper cup with a rolled lip, Elliott noticed that Miranda, in addition to carefully spraying and brushing back her expensively cut hair, had applied tiny, barely visible lines of paint between her lower lashes. How, he thought, could a woman on the way to her daughter's deathbed summon the presence of mind to apply the most elaborate of makeup tricks, the kind meant, he supposed, to fool the eye for black-tie occasions? And dress so carefully, her stockings matching her low-heeled shoes, her shoes matching her bag?

Was this simply how Miranda managed not to fly to bits?

"I thought," he began, and stopped.

"You thought," she prompted him.

Elliott pulled Amelia onto his lap. She lay back against him. "I want a water," Amelia said.

Elliott let Amelia sip some of his lukewarm, sugary tea.

"Won't that keep her up?"

"She's not going to go to sleep anyhow." Elliott shrugged.

"I want a pee wee," Amelia said. Elliott took Amelia into the antiseptic washroom, with its high high seat. "I don't want to get on that. It will die me," she said.

"You won't fall in. Daddy will hold you," Elliott said.

"I want Mama, though," Amelia said apologetically. Elliott thought, Should I get Laura? Would she be touched, perhaps too much, at the humble sweetness of this task? But suddenly, as Amelia clung to his arms, Elliott heard a few drops flow. "Go ahead, honey," said Elliott. "Go on and let the wee out." For some reason, the tensile grip of Amelia's arms brought home to him the enormity of his life's cataclysmic change. An empty bed. A single line of pairs of shoes. Drawers and drawers filled with no scarves and unmated socks and a shower rod without bras drying, like miniature banners, on rows of hangers. Turning off the alarm, alone, waking in the dark, without Laura, like a heat-seeking missile, having nudged her firm butt against his back, until he literally was over the edge of his side of the bed. Would the day still bloom without Laura's sleepy murmur, "Time to make the doughnuts, Ell. Time to hit the deck." Athena's whining growl of awakening, as she rose, hind end first, from her pad on the floor. The smell of Antonia's Flowers, the bottle he gave her every Christmas. Would the grass grow now that they would no longer bicker about who'd mowed it last? Would the sun rise now that they could no longer beg each other to get up and make the oatmeal and give the other just five more precious minutes of sleep before the onslaught of the day? Carpooling and dinners, school forms—he and Laura joked that school for three children generated more paperwork than the Pentagon—all on him, all for him, all without Laura to remind him that none of it mattered, that tomorrow would be soon enough? Amelia looked up at him with her widely spaced, always tentative gray eyes.

"It's okay," he told her. "Everything will be okay."

He washed Amelia's hands between his own and dried them on a cheap, nonabsorbent paper towel. Why give people in crisis such short shrift? he thought. Why not pillows, blankets . . . muffins?

He supposed such niceties were reserved for the birthing rooms, the places where relatives waited for good tidings.

"You were going to say . . ." His mother-in-law ambushed him when he and Amelia emerged.

"I wondered what you had told the girls," he finally said, "so I would know later."

Miranda sighed. "I wasn't going to tell them anything, but Annie asked right away if her mother was very sick, and of course then it was how sick, and then it was who would look after them . . ."

"All this on the way from Natick?"

"I'm sure you can explain things better later on," Miranda told him. "I certainly didn't volunteer anything they didn't ask."

"That's good."

Miranda sighed again. "Her father . . . Laura's

father." She sighed in reverse, a long, repentant, inward breath, but her expression—so far as Elliott could tell—was not fond but exasperated. "He'd fallen in the shower and cut himself shaving. I heard him fall, or Suzie did, and I thought it was the cut that made him so woozy; he was bleeding. They *stitched the cut.* Can you imagine? He died four hours later."

"I suspect they thought he'd live, even if he were impaired somehow."

"They may have; but that's not what they told us," Miranda said decisively.

"So you feel as though you've been through this."

"I don't mean this as an insult to you, Elliott, but however much you love your husband, it can never feel the same as losing your child. Your child dying. I still don't believe that it will happen. I keep thinking the surgeon will find some . . . some way. I can't look at her, sitting there all shiny and with her hair brushed, and make that square with her being fatally ill. Dying while we watch, helpless to do anything for her."

Elliott said, "He said there was no hope. Doctor

Campanile. Virtually. That we could put her on life support to harvest her organs."

"You refused that."

"No. It's what she wants."

"Elliott, that's . . . beastly. Don't you think it actually encourages doctors not to try as hard?" Miranda asked. "That's what Juliet thinks." Juliet was Miranda's younger sister.

"This doctor is a pretty square shooter."

Rory, her eyes rubbed nearly raw, walked into the room and asked for a Pepsi. Elliott fished in his pockets and gave her a dollar in change.

Rory sat down. "It's exhausting me," she said solemnly.

"And so it should," Miranda told her granddaughter. "You are very brave, Aurora Miranda."

Rory leaned against Elliott's knee. She felt immense, weighty, her sixty sprightly pounds a limp mass. "Dad," she said.

"Hey?" Elliott hugged her, subtly shifting her weight from his tingling knee.

"Are we going to have to sell our car? And our house? Because Mommy died?"

"No, who told you that?"

"Caitlin Carver's mother got divorced and she had to sell their house."

"Oh, Rory. Mommy and I aren't getting divorced. We've never been mad at each other like that and we never would be. We won't have to sell our house. Everything in our house will stay just the same. Don't worry, baby girl."

"How about the dog? She eats, like, ten pounds of food a week. We'll have to sell Athena . . ."

"We won't have to sell Athena." Rory kicked off her shoes and padded out into the hall to the pop machine. "Dad?" she asked softly, glancing back in. "Am I going to have to quit?"

"Quit what?"

"The gym? I know how expensive it is, and Mom says I'm ready for private lessons, but you don't have to get them for me . . ."

"We'll have to . . . figure things out," Elliott said. "It'll be all right." Rory left the room, and they heard her drop the quarters, then the clang of her pop can hitting the tray. "Why is she thinking about selling the dog?" he wondered aloud, half to Miranda and half to himself.

"Children do," Miranda said. "They did, mine, when their father died. They were going to . . . Elliott, you certainly can tell me to shut my mouth if you wish to, but I have been here. Mine, they were going to hold a garage sale and sell their old clothes because they were afraid of the very same sort of things. It wasn't exactly selfish. It's not exactly as though they're self-centered . . . it's more as though they're programmed for self-preservation first . . . I can't explain."

"You'd think they'd think of nothing but their mother."

"But Laura looks the same to them as she always did. She hasn't lost her hair, or been in a wheelchair . . . how can you expect them to grasp how sick she is?" Miranda asked, and then added, "You *are* okay, aren't you?"

"My wife is dying," Elliott told her, shocked. "How can I be okay? I'm not sobbing and screaming, but . . ."

How am I, Elliott thought? I'm an idiot buying cards that say "Way to Go, Graduate!" I'm a flatliner, trotting around on the tile.

"I mean, are you okay financially?"

"What . . . ? How can *you* bring that up? Or, more to the point, only you *would* bring that up, Miranda. Now, of all times."

"Because I care. I can help, that way. Do you really have enough to take care of them? Without Laura's income?"

"Actually, we have very good insurance. Laura insisted."

"That's very odd. Her income was not significant."

"It was a big help. It paid for the girls' lessons. As for the insurance. Laura wanted to get it while we were younger because the premiums were cheaper. And it was like an investment. For the girls. We did it years ago."

"Mmmm," Miranda mused. "It's almost as if she had a presentiment."

"No, Miranda, it's almost as if she thought we could get low rates, and it would be an investment A savings account we couldn't touch every time one of the kids wanted a GameBoy."

"Well, what has it . . . how has it done?"

"We should realize . . . a couple of hundred thousand. Or more."

"That won't go far."

"*A hundred thousand dollars*?" Rory cried. Elliott and Miranda started. They exchanged perhaps the first synchronic gaze in their entire acquaintance: Nothing Rory said would make either of them rebuke her. "We'll be rich! We'll be as rich as the Priors or the Wisens! We could put in a pool!"

The price being one mother, Elliott thought, giving Miranda a poisonous smile, which she did not deserve. "We won't be as rich as the Priors or the Wisens and we aren't putting in a pool because Amelia can't even swim and could fall in, and . . ." He could not stop himself. "Rory, I can't believe you just said that."

"What?" Rory asked.

Elliott sighed. Rory had no sense of the social vice comprised by mentioning money in the same breath with death, the awkward cross-tied position of the heir. Though shocked by his child's naked materialism, he knew mortal irrevocability was still unreal for Rory. Someone at work had once told him that children grieved in reverse, that while adults were stricken sharply at once and slowly recovered, children were initially blasé, but the longer the loved person was absent, they experienced greater recognition of loss.

He and Miranda watched Rory wander back to her mother's room. Simultaneously, Miranda and Elliott released deep breaths.

"We actually would be quite flush by our standards, Miranda," Elliott said abruptly. "I *thought* you were asking if I was *doing okay.*" A hatred so foul and sizzling it felt like internal combustion gripped Elliott's gut; he was surprised Miranda did not feel it lick out and scorch her composed face.

"Well, good," Miranda complimented him. "What Rory said is normal, Elliott. Children want to know what's going to happen to them. They can't grieve if they're afraid that their beds will be taken away. I know that much."

"How are *you,* Miranda? Are you okay?"

"I'm not stupid," Miranda said, opening the clasp on her bag, extracting a perfectly clean handkerchief. "I know you're asking how I feel about Laurie. She's my child. I expected her to outlive me by many, many years. I suppose I'm in shock."

"But you didn't act that way while she was alive," Elliott interrupted. "God!" He slapped his forehead. "I mean, during our marriage." He could not believe his audacity. No one living ever spoke this way to Miranda. "You weren't *motherly*. Or *grandmotherly*. You *agreed* to come on holidays. That's not all there is to it. You didn't . . . call for no reason. Do you know you never once had the girls stay overnight?"

"But I worked at night . . ."

"You didn't have to . . ."

"I did, and also . . ."

"You just found it easier to deal with perfect strangers and make their dreams come true than to deal with your own children," Elliott said thickly, aware this would have none but an ill effect and disgusted with himself for saying it. "Don't you see what a mess Stephen is? That he lives like a college boy?"

"We had card parties," Miranda said.

"Card parties?"

"And charades. And the children would play, oh, whatever they did, hide-and-seek, outside in summer, that game with the flashlights . . . hordes of them, cousins and kids from the block."

"Ghosts in the Graveyard," Elliott told her, suddenly cold.

"We would have these get-togethers, when Stephen Senior was alive. We'd make a bowl of punch, rum, and apple cider. All of us were so poor. My sister, Juliet, and Stephen's friend Jimmy from work, and his wife, she was Greek." Miranda went on, "I can remember us literally rolling up the rug in the old house, to dance. We have old eight-millimeter movies of us dancing . . ."

"And after?"

"I honestly tried. I remember a Fourth of July barbecue I tried to put together. I burned my eyelashes off starting the grill."

"I don't know what this has to do with how you were to your own children . . ."

"I didn't know how to do things! How to do the things to keep their lives the same. You'll have to do that, Elliott . . . ," Miranda said, her face flushed.

"I will," he said stoutly.

"Take care you do, because otherwise . . . nobody invited us, Elliott," Miranda said. "A widow with four children is not an asset to a gathering. And I suppose they were naughty. Stevie was. Angela was."

"Why didn't you just read to them? Listen to the same music as you had before, with Stephen Senior? Watch the home movies, together?"

Miranda folded her hands. "Well, Elliott, I suppose I was afraid it would hurt me too much," said Miranda. "To be honest, I did not feel the same. I didn't feel like doing the same things. I could always say I was busy. With work."

*A widow with four children is not an asset,* Elliott thought.

* * *

With Rory nestled beside her, fiddling with the dials on the bedside radio, Laura told her daughter that she knew how it felt to want to be the most popular one. "I was that way, too. I would try to tie my scarves around my neck—we all wore these little silk scarves the size of a bandana, but wrapped around with little clips on them, and I could never get them right. I would try to tie them on for forty minutes in the morning, until the scarf was filthy and damp from my hands, and then I go to school, and there was Petty DiCastro, with hers tied just like on the video in JC Penney's. They had this little TV you could watch to learn how to tie the scarves once you bought one." Rory had been the child to whom Laura could prattle forever. She always seemed interested and made appropriate comments no matter how far off the path Laura strayed. "What I mean is, I tried too hard to fit in, until I found my sport. What I want you to do, even if you don't stay in the gym, is try very hard not to be that kind of person even for a little while." Rory nodded vigorously. "Do you know what I mean? The kind of person someone popular can talk into anything? Once, the popular girls—there were four of them, and they wore a knot in their shoes tied exactly the same way—talked me into standing on the edge of Rat Prairie . . . you don't know where Rat Prairie is, do you? I suppose Rat Prairie isn't even there anymore; it's condos. But it was named for what was in it. Anyhow, while they went in there and made out with their boyfriends in the tall grass, someone set a fire, and the rats came running out. The fire department came. I was the one there. They took me to the station. I was hysterical. It was the most horrible thing I ever saw, the rats, Rory, like in the Pied Piper . . ." Why am I rambling, Laura wondered. Is it because of what is going on in my head? No, she thought ruefully, I always rambled. I could never get to the point. Elliott called it backing around the corner to the beginning.

Was *that,* she thought, because of what was wrong in my head, even then?

"Rory, listen." Laura willfully gathered her thoughts and tucked Rory's small shoulder under her own arm as they reclined on the bed. "Are you listening to me? Nothing, no matter how much it matters at the time, is worth doing something you think is wrong. And you always know."

"How?" Rory asked.

"You ask the still, small voice, like Father Delabue said," Laura told Rory. "And if you feel a doubt, that's your real self telling you what to do, always."

"Even if it's telling you to be afraid," Rory ventured.

Laura sighed. It was foolish, and Laura knew it to be foolish, to try to impart an encyclopedia of mothering into a spare few minutes. But a spare few minutes were her lot. She could not protect Rory from her eager, anxious personality, from being the child who knew the birthdays of everyone else in her class so she could mourn in advance to which parties she wouldn't be invited. That was a mother's job—They're only jealous of you, sweetheart. When you're older, they'll all want to be your friend—all the ready, hopeful falsehoods of parenthood. Perhaps they were jealous? Perhaps Rory really simply was a late bloomer, as Laura had been? She could not confer goodness and confidence on Rory like a healing, like the prophylactic

antibiotics she'd given her for troublesome earaches when Rory was a baby. She could only give Rory a memory, and it had better be a sufficient one.

"Well, like now, of course, it's natural you should be afraid," Laura told her. "That's simply recognizing your own real feelings." But Laura also reminded her daughter to think of all the times fear could be a trickster, the times Rory'd cried before meets, terrified she would fall on the beam and hurt herself or—worse, for Rory—foul her routine, and how many times she had gone ahead and done it despite her fears, and done it perfectly, landed it perfectly.

"Should I write this down?" Rory asked.

"I wrote it down for you."

"Will you be our guardian angel?"

"If I can." Laura caught her breath at the sharp veer of the questioning. "Of course I will. But Rory, here's a secret. Even if I die, you can see the best part of me again. When you get to be forty"—Rory's eyes widened—"you do this. You look down at your hands, and you'll see my hands. You're the one who looks just like me, except your pretty curly red hair. You'll see my hands because your hands will have grown to look just like mine."

"I won't make regionals," Rory mourned, "because I'll be emotionally disturbed." Laura thought, and grimly, of her mother's misplaced candor, on the drive from Natick. Her mother would go ahead with her champagne brunch. Laura's funeral would have to wait.

"Yes, you will make regionals," Laura told her daughter firmly. "People go on after horrible things happen and it actually makes them better at whatever they do. You know how Father Delabue always says, when you're sad, offer it up? That's how you do it. You offer it up."

"To Jesus?"

Hell, thought Laura. "No, to Mama," she said, holding tiny Rory against her with all her strength. "I will always be your mama, Rory. I will always be inside you."

"I don't believe in Santa," said Rory. "Anymore. Will Santa come?"

"Absolutely. Why would Santa punish you because your mom got sick?"

"Well, I'll have to miss a lot of school," Rory concluded, her face finally dry, but swollen as a plum.

"That's right," Laura said. 'Tis an ill wind, she thought.

Elliott and Miranda sat knee to knee, Elliott's jeans nearly touching the sharp camel crease of Miranda's slacks. Miranda accepted a copy of the *Globe* from a passing volunteer in pink. Now, Elliott thought, *she's going to read the paper?* She said, "You'll have to make sure they keep in touch with Suzie's children and Angela's . . ."

"Why don't *you, too*?" Elliott cried. "You're the matriarch. You have the house on the Cape. Why didn't you build a little compound with guest cottages at the shore? Why don't you now, in light of this? Why don't *you* preserve the extended family?"

Guest cottages, he thought. That's a little Kennedy.

Asking a bit much. "Why didn't you at least reassure them, all the time, back then? Why don't you make a resolution to do it now?"

"Well, Suzie was almost a teenager when Stephen died, and she wasn't much interested in things like that . . ."

"She was nine, Miranda! No bigger than Rory. Laura and Angie were little. Angie was practically a baby. I'm sorry for this, but my own father has done a basically crap job with the girls . . . and so has my sister. It's not only you."

Good God, he realized then, I haven't called my father. Or my sister.

He glanced at his watch. The time was flooding past; it was already morning, breakfast time on school days. Nurses were hailing one another, wishing one another good holidays. Elliott realized his time with Laura was collapsing slowly, like a spent parachute—that his life A.D. was about to commence. And there had been no time, to tell her how he had never, at a party, lusted for another woman, how he had never felt anything but lucky to glance across the room at his innocent little imp in her one fancy black dress, Laura's mittened hand so trustingly on the crook of his elbow, Laura grimly instructing him that he couldn't chisel cost when it came to perennials, that one box of sedum was not enough to fill in the cracks in a wall, Laura learning the tango from a videotape and becoming furious when she couldn't teach him, Laura. Laura!

But he would not know, not for days, during the bustle of the funeral, the parade of the casseroles, that eventually time would grind down to a slow-motion dressage of seconds and minutes to be hurdled. That time would change character, from the headlong gallop of family life to a grim march. Seconds would become weeks, weeks centuries, for months to come. He would glance at calendars and be stunned to see that it was still February, that his tragedy, like a weight he needed virtually to strap onto his back and carry with him wherever he went, had grown no less heavy, so he could not even begin the process of speeding up, of trying to outdistance it. The weight would confer its own terms, its own tenancy.

He would have the sense to avoid paging through

photo albums; but he would not be able to stop the flip-book in his head—of the moments wasted because they were presumed infinite, the nights two tired young parents had contented themselves with a pat instead of a tumble, turned their backs to each other—*turned their backs!*—and gone to sleep gratefully, in the utter certainty that each of them would have another chance, tomorrow, or Saturday morning. All those chances had been wadded into a sloppy ball and tossed away for him by an indifferent fate.

Miranda's lips were moving. Elliott had to wrest himself down into the room to concentrate on her words. "I was off there, distracted," he apologized. "Tell me again what you just said."

"I loved them," Miranda offered uncertainly. "You should know. I loved them. My sister and I didn't come from a family where you got hugged and kissed just for coming through the door. Stephen Senior did. And his parents were always petting and patting him, too. Like your mother." Elliott thought briefly of his own mother, her careless tousles, her habit of massaging his neck, once annoying, now longed for. "How was I to change . . . ?"

Elliott drew a deep breath. "You have time, Miranda. I'd take it. You know, Laura doesn't think that you love her. She doesn't think you're proud of her. She thinks you're proud of Angela and that you love only Suzanne."

"That's absurd." Miranda silenced him, her fingers absently braiding Amelia's hair.

"I know it's horrible to tell you. But while she can still understand you, you might say something, for your own sake . . . she doesn't really know how her sisters and brothers grew up so close . . ."

What Miranda said next, Elliott would remember one day, years later, when he'd chased Annie down the hall so furiously that he'd run into the wallboard over the laundry chute, nearly breaking his nose, leaving a mark that would remain for years. Annie had told him to shut his fat mouth when he grounded her after she was caught sneaking Rory out of the house at midnight to meet boys at the gazebo.

All those years later, he would confide in Miranda that during their confrontation at the hospital, he truly had not realized how very hard it would be, how friendships would grow slim, then dim, then brittle and sparse. Abashed, he would apologize—over coffee he had learned to brew with delicate expertise—for his hysterical and presumptuous suggestion that she start a family *compound.* And with reticence and tolerance, she would assure him that the addition she'd built onto the cottage, after Laura died, was no accident. She would assure Elliott that, for all his mistakes, he had done what she had not—bound the girls to him as well as to one another, not only with unqualified love but with the tireless expression of it. And Elliott would recall exactly what Miranda had said to him, her defense against his barrage. She'd said, "I think I was afraid they'd turn away. That they'd always liked Stephen Senior better. *And* they had each other, and that is really how it is supposed to be, Elliott. It's supposed to be them against us."

It would turn out to be the best advice anyone would ever give him, and it would see him through those times when both Annie and Rory assured him that they fervently wished he had died instead of their mother.

But that night, when neither of them could back off, they were both relieved to be drawn off the subject by the sound of pounding feet. Angela, her scarf and coat thickly frosted with wet snow, flew past the quiet-room door on her way to pop into every room on the hall until she found Laura. Cobb, her fiancé, stopped to shrug at Elliott and Miranda. "We barely got into Logan. It's closed now," he said. "We got a flight at six A.M." In his hands he held a large, lifelike stuffed Scottie, a plaid bow about its neck. Amelia got up from the floor and took it from him, tucking it under her arm with a businesslike air, as if she understood that this was her duty, the beginning of her acceptance of homages.

After Angela had cried herself to sleep in the hard leather chair, Laura finally allowed herself to feel tired. She would not let herself sleep; but she lay back and burrowed into the blankets, glad of the downy yielding cuddling of the bed jacket. To her dread, she was beginning to feel cold, cold even to the touch.

Just as she had settled, Elliott tried to bring Amelia in. The tot screamed and hid her face in Elliott's sweater. "She was asking for you, really," Elliott told Laura. His face, in the room's artificial light, was nearly lavender.

"It's okay, Ell, she's scared," Laura told him with resignation. "She doesn't get all this sadness over me just sitting here."

"But you have to hold her. You have to hold her now, and touch her." Elliott was desperate to protect both daughter and wife.

"I won't have any memory and neither will she," Laura told him firmly, almost heartlessly, as her mother walked into the room, with Laura's brother, Stephen. Stephen, in a sweater and a stupid Sherlock Holmes hat half unraveled, was soaked to the skin. Angela awoke and cried out his name, but Stephen gazed, levelly, quietly observant, into Laura's eyes, as

Angela clung to him around the knees from her seat near the bed.

"My car died," he said.

"It's the night for it," Laura told him.

"Do you want to talk to Laura alone?" Miranda asked her son.

"For one moment," said Stephen. He cupped Laura's chin in his hands. "Sissy," he said.

"Come and wash your face, Angela," Miranda told her.

"I don't want to leave." Angela was awake and freshly primed to cry.

"Come and have a glass of water and wash your face," Miranda said, and Angela, her snow-clotted scarf still hanging from the neck of her sweater, followed. Looking back as if in afterthought, she took Rory's hand and picked up Amelia. "Come on, Rory glory," Angela said. "Is your ACL still strained?"

"I don't think so," Rory said, sticking out one leg, displaying her knobby knee with its ropy muscled thigh. "I lifted weights."

"I'll check it," Angela told her.

And Laura had a sudden preview of how life would be, as if she'd been scissored out of a picture—a space, yes, there would always be an empty space, but with life proceeding, smiles and warnings, encouragement and endearments exchanged around and through her.

Life.

"Get my credit card out of my purse, Stevie," Laura told him.

He did, and did not ask why. "Ell is going to forget where the presents are, though I wrote it all down for him. They're in the closet behind the boiler. You're going to forget, too. I love Ell because he is so much like you, not in any way that people would notice. In ways only I notice." She watched, with a nearly dispassionate pity, as Stephen's eyes filled. "What I want you to do is give me a kiss and then go out and buy everything you can. Solid gold jewelry for Annie. Weights and a portable chinning bar for Rory, and expensive soap for both of them. The real creamy stuff, in teenager boxes. And boom boxes. And get Amelia one of those little cars that a kid can really sit in that goes on its own. And those twin babies that ask for ice cream . . ."

"Wait," he said. "Do you have a pen?" Carefully, he wrote down every item Laura named.

"Then scatter it all under the tree. Everywhere. And take the price tags off. Please take the price tags *off.* I ask you this with all my heart. And . . . and please get married, Stephen. I can't take care of you anymore. You can't call me on the phone and tell me you just had sex with the backup singer for Pat Benatar. Please find a good woman and get married. And look after Elliott. And Anna. *Annie.* She's changing her name."

"That already is her name," Stephen said, his unruly hair crimping from the moisture. He seemed apologetic, as if loath to point out Laura's infirmity.

"No, no! She's changing it to Annie Laurie," Laura said, with more irritation than she meant to betray or to feel. Stephen let his face drop into his hands. For a moment, Laura thought he was angry; but he was touched beyond ordinary tolerance. Surely transmitting these revelations must be far worse than dying, Laura thought. She had never been subjected to the battery of so much unadulterated grief. She knew people who wondered idly what it would be like to be at their own funerals. She knew she would not have been able to bear the poignancy of her own. She had hoped to ask Elliott to have the organist play "Silent Night" at her mass; it was, after all, a hymn. Her favorite. But she found herself unable to bring up the topic of the days ahead.

"I'll see she gets the name thing done," Stephen said.

"Elliott won't mind. He'll be in a forgiving mood."

"Sis, will you . . . when I come back?"

"I don't know. They said eight or twelve hours. I've been talking nonstop for eight hours. It can't be so much longer."

"So I could be at the goddamned Toys R Us when you die?"

"Stevie. Would you really rather be here?" Laura asked, as abruptly her mind heaved and thrust upward, as if an earthquake had occurred beneath her bed. She bucked. There was nowhere to cling.

She saw Angela, her fairy-princess wedding gown spread like a lily on the bank as she knelt near some body of water, all three of Laura's girls in identical outfits of some rosy fabric, arrayed about her like petals, Stephen in tails, with a woman so tiny she appeared to be Vietnamese, Thai, in a lovely sage dress, cut on the bias, gazing up at him. She saw her own mother, reading to Amelia, a slightly larger and blonder Amelia, from a leather-covered book; she could not see the title, but Miranda's face was more animated than Laura had ever seen it, her careful avoidance of excessive smiles and frowns neglected as she made expressions for what apparently mimed the cruel witch and the frightened child. She saw Suzie, a head shorter than a tall and angular Aaron, Aaron was wearing sailing clothes, sport racing clothes. More water. An ocean twinkled behind them, in the yard of a house that looked like her mom's summer home, but with a big porch and a garage apartment. She saw Elliott, walking away from her . . .

Laura surfaced, gasping, in her hospital room.

Stephen and Amelia sat beside her. "Elliott couldn't watch," Stephen said.

"I begged you to go, hours ago," Laura told Stephen.

"Grow what?" Stephen asked. "Grow up?"

"I begged you to go to store," Laura said, irritated.

"We're not at the shore, Sis. You're in the hospital. Don't you remember? You had a . . . seizure, about five minutes ago."

"Did she see?" Laura asked Stephen.

"We're not at the shore," Stephen said.

Amelia, her great, wildly lashed eyes tip-tilted, said, "Mama have a tummy ache."

"Yes, baby," Laura answered. She opened her arms, and Amelia came into them, promptly clutching Laura's ear and falling asleep.

"You can't understand what she says," Stephen told Elliott. Why did he not leave? Her children would have no Christmas.

"What time is it?" she asked.

"She'll be here soon," Elliott told her. "She's on her way from the airport. She had to drive from Providence." Laura glanced at the window. The sky was darkening. Or was it? She had no idea of the time.

But it was Christmas Eve. This was Christmas for Laura, the anticipation before the satiation, the formality and delicacy. A night of fine fabrics and fine food, and mass at midnight, receiving the wafer.

"In the Name of the Father, and of the Son, and of the Holy Spirit," said Father Delabue.

No, it was not Father Delabue. It was a priest she did not recognize—a tiny man, brown hair grizzled to clay-tipped gray. "Daughter of the Lord, sinless through baptism, your earthly sins are forgiven, your passage to heaven . . ."

"She will choke on this," said Dr. Campanile. The wafer was a hoof in Laura's mouth.

"Annie told me that when she was dying, she almost really did die," Rory said.

Where was the priest?

"The oil is sufficient and more than sufficient," the priest said then.

"She saw a man in a railroad hat and striped blue jeans," Rory went on. "Do you hear me, Mama? With red hair under his hat."

Laura said, "Yes. Are you sure?"

"She's here," Elliott told her. "You spoke to Suzie."

"Stephen?"

"She's *here,* Laura. And Angie is here."

"I drove from Providence," Suzie said, and Laura saw Aaron's pale, preternaturally mature small face, his white hand tentatively lifted, waving at her from the doorway. She raised her hand and made the okay sign with her fingers. A brief, pinched grin crossed Aaron's face.

". . . that I was a bad mother, not loving enough, but I was so frightened. I had to work all hours for you four," Miranda said, "but I do love you. I did love you. I'm proud of you, Laurie, for being the mother I was not."

"I know," Laura said.

"Please don't say no," Miranda pleaded. "Don't say that."

"Laurie! Laurie!" Angie was shaking her shoulder, then holding her underwater. Laura tried to shrug Angela's hand loose, then to tear away her sister's strong fingers, and finally came up and gulped for breath.

". . . a ventilator, in a short time," said Dr. Campanile. Elliott, tiny and dark-ringed in a corner of the room, shook his head, then nodded sadly.

"There hasn't been many time for us to be saying things poems and important to talk over which meant to us that you were always my deficits," said Elliott.

Laura shook her head. "Elliott, we talked about important things every day, for fourteen years."

"I suppose because I don't want to frighten Amelia even more," he said. "There will be plenty of time for tears. Or did you mean fear?"

Stephen was leaning over her, his smell unmistakable. "I did it all," he said, "and you held on. Everything is under the tree, Sis. I love you, Sis. I love you more than I love my own life. I wish to merciful . . ."

"God have mercy on the soul of Laura MacDermott Banner, and carry her from strength into strength," said Father Delabue, surely he this time. Laura imagined she lay in a bed made for a Cleopatra, padded in silver and rose, her mother standing at her feet, wearing a black mantilla and the highest heels, the image of the older Jackie Kennedy, her bobbed hair black with violet undertones.

"No!" cried Amelia. "Mama eye open."

She was still in the hospital. Amelia had awakened

in her arms. Or had she? Was Amelia really beside her? She reached for Amelia, and all that filled her hungry arms was a pillow. Angels sang "*Adeste fideles. Venite adoramus,*" and "I Heard the Bells on Christmas Day."

"The nurses are singing. They do sound like the angels," Dr. Campanile told Laura, who was unaware that she had spoken. "Christmas at my work is the saddest day. And this is the saddest of all of the Christmases I have spent at my work. You have the loveliest young girls. You have named the red-haired little one Aurora."

"Yes. Thank you," Laura said. "We wanted them all to match. All beginning with *A*. It seems silly now, to have thought that would matter, having it all fit in the right way."

"She seems very bright indeed," the doctor told her. "I don't know whether it will make it more hard or more easy. I think they will all do well. They have your soul, I think."

"I don't know, either," Laura said, "but I am ready."

"Can you see, Laura?"

"Not very well," she replied.

"Is there any pain?"

"No. Are my girls here?"

"Elliott has taken the bambina, but Rory was here talking about the railroad man." Laura felt her hand lifted, a finger against her fluttering pulse. "In a while, we will insert a tube to help you breathe, so you don't have to work so hard . . ."

"Why," Laura said suddenly, struggling to rise in the bed, "that was my grandfather! The man Annie saw! My grandfather was a railroad engineer. He died in a fire. That is the man with the red hair! We never could figure out why Rory had reddish hair! I remember him now! I barely knew him, but he was so kind."

"Perhaps you will see him," said Dr. Campanile. "Perhaps he is there now, holding his lantern."

Laura tried to smirk at his sentimentality, but her lips would not obey. She pointed at them, and then her chest, pushing away the pillows, drowning, thrashing. A nurse and the doctor pried apart her teeth, and Laura obediently swallowed—a good girl, swallowing what she was told—her throat slack. She tried to see faces through the lambent light of candles carried in a row. She squinted. There was Elliott, his shirt stuck all over with her notes, his pockets bulging with more; he put his lips against her brow. "I don't think I can bear it," he said. "Laura, my own Laura, no!" With one finger, Laura tapped his hand. It was not her concern anymore. Not for this moment. She had to work at this next step.

"I think everyone can come now," the doctor said, and Laura felt rather than saw all of them swoop down upon her, buoying her up, over the coved roof of the hospital, helping her reach up so that she might garb herself in stars. She could hear the nurses singing, "Silent night, holy night," for long moments after Dr. Campanile pronounced aloud the time on the clock.

One day in July, when the hot-water heater gave out with a horrible bleat, Elliott went rummaging to find the source of the problem and came upon the stack of wrapped and named Christmas presents in the tiny closet off the downstairs bath.

There was a ski sweater for him, and a screened T-shirt of all the girls, tumbled about him on the sand at Cape Cod. There was a gift certificate for CDRah, the music store.

Hesitating, he called the girls and gave them their boxes. Annie set off for her room, but Elliott demanded she sit down with the others.

"Oh, ritual," Annie sneered, "I forgot the importance of ritual!"

She fingered her stack of books and the cashmere sweater she had once admired so extravagantly in a store window. She said that it felt to her as though it would itch her skin; Elliott might wish to give it to Goodwill. And it was too hot to try on a sweater; the very thought made her nauseated. But she cradled the music box, which had individual perforated discs and played classical tunes. The inlay on the lid she did think was pretty, a Scottish rose.

Rory had grown, and the fancy leotard and sweat suit no longer fit her. But there was a locket—Elliott found this spooky, precognitive—containing a lock of Laura's and Elliott's hair with one of Rory's baby curls like a swirl of bright thread in the center. And the perfume was her mother's favorite. Rory would hoard it—even after years of baby-sitting when she could have purchased many bottles with her own money—placing a drop each night on her pillow. She would make it last for five years. Each time she competed, she would rub a drop into her wrist braces. Not the first year after Laura's death but the second, she placed first on the beam in regionals; and the third year, third at nationals. She remained tiny, never, even in adulthood, topping five feet one.

When Amelia opened her boxes, the Amish doll family her mother had carefully mail-ordered frightened her, because the dolls had eyes but no mouths or noses. She was captivated, though, by the set of colored pencils, crayons, and paint, in a case with her very own initials on it, which she could now read. She began to draw in her sketchbook daily, and in time she'd make a human figure that would astound her kindergarten teacher with its detail and perspective.

Late in October, while searching for a pack of matches to light the first fire of the season far too early, because the girls wanted to watch Halloween movies by its light, Elliott opened the nightstand that had held Laura's reading glasses and her manicure kit, long since given to her pals, along with most of her clothing. He would have searched her desk, where he knew she kept a haphazard collection of restaurant matches for gas stove emergencies and birthday candles. But Suzanne had taken Laura's desk, insisted on shipping it to her own home in San Diego the very day after the funeral, despite the ghost it left on the wall, which had forced Elliott to repaint the whole room. There was nothing in the drawer, but in a lower paneled compartment he never opened, he found a novel, neatly marked with a clean Popsicle stick, and a silver box with a card.

His gift was a fine Belle Temps watch with two circlets on a single clock face, one set accurately to Boston time, one many hours later. He opened the card and read some lines he recognized vaguely from a college English course, Elizabeth Barrett counting the depths and breadths of her love for her husband. Inside, Laura had written, "Guess what time it is in

Paris?" and signed her name within the outline of a heart.

Three years later, after Elliott had established trusts for all the girls' educations and had paid off Angela's student loans, he found he had substantial investments and disposable income. He had never suspected to enter midlife without dire financial strangling. Genuinely, and for the first time without a tweak of guilt, he was gladdened by the size of the insurance policy they had purchased, costly and improbably useful as it had seemed so long ago, as well as the drudgery he had given the plant in exchange for profit shares.

And so, he took the girls to Paris.

At the last moment before they headed for the airport bus, Elliott halted the cab and rushed back into the house, reaching high into his armoire, into the pottery jar painted with orange roses, a wedding gift so revolting they'd kept it for humor's sake. He scooped out a handful of ash, crumbling, the color of lead, the consistency of potting soil, and slipped it into a plastic zip bag he snagged from the kitchen drawer.

Late on the second day, they approached the Eiffel Tower, and Amelia, six and sassy, asked, "Do they have a levelator? Because I'm not crawling up *that*!"

Annie tried to pretend she had been forced to visit a landmark with a group of perfect strangers.

"Dad, look at the line," pragmatic Rory said softly. "It's, like, a block long . . . and I'm starving . . . couldn't we come back another time? We're going to be here . . ."

"How about never?" Annie suggested. "How about we come back never? I mean, let's go up in the Eiffel Tower . . . how very original!"

"Look, Anna," Elliott began.

"Ann-eeeee!" his daughter pounced. "Hello! Pleased to meet you; I'm your daughter, and I'm also, pardon me, the only one who ever thinks about her anyhow, so this whole tribute to my father's long-lost love kind of sucks . . ."

"That's not true!" Rory shouted. "I think about her all the time!"

"Oh, yes, little Miss Cathy Rigby? How many Saturdays have I had to sit on a hard bleacher seat listening to 'Eye of the Tiger' umpteen times while a bunch of little anorexics did their floor exercise?"

"You . . . you." Rory glanced at Amelia. "You butt wipe, Annie! You think that because you're the oldest, you loved her better."

"I think I knew her! I don't think any of you did!"

"Shut up!" Elliott shouted, hideously embarrassed for the two elderly couples who jumped and grabbed for each other's hands. He lowered his voice. "Annie, you can stay down here and . . . and use the cell phone to call your lousy hoodlum friends"—Annie snorted—"if you want; but Rory and Amelia and I are going to go up there, and yeah, forgive me if I haven't had . . . the heart to talk about Mom every day since she's been gone, not because I don't miss her but *because* I miss her like hell . . . or the time to tell you stories about her every day, partially because you've done everything in your power to make my life a constant effort to keep you out of juvenile detention."

"Don't blame me because you just couldn't wait to repaint the bedroom."

"Your mother and I had one of the best marriages I ever knew of, Annie! I hope you get lucky enough to have one as good yourself!" Elliott snapped, taking the two younger girls by their hands and taking his place at the end of the line, glancing at the lowering sun and hoping his private ritual would not have to be postponed by Annie's tantrum. "Try not to get kidnapped while we're up there!"

While they waited, Elliott trying to recover his breath and reading to the girls about the history of the structure from a pamphlet, giving them each bites of the single chocolate bar he had, Annie made an elaborate pantomime of stomping off, inspecting a whirling kiosk of postcards, applying her lip gloss—all the while glancing at Elliott to make sure he noticed her indifference. At last, with a huge sigh, she joined them, folding her arms and facing away from her family, at the remove of a couple of yards, in the queue.

When they finally reached the top of the elaborate web, Elliott had not even the chance to take out his camera before he literally ran into a woman who was busy trying to control her short skirt, straw hat, and carryall. "Be careful!" she cried. "*S'il vous plaît!* You'll knock me off!"

"There are strong fences. Don't be afraid. I'm an American," Elliott said.

"I'm afraid of heights," the woman confided. "I'm also an American. I've crept along the edge of every monument in Europe. Why do I do it? I keep thinking I'll conquer my fear. I never do. And I understand irrational fear. I see it in my work every day. If there had been the slightest breeze, I wouldn't have come up here at all!"

Yet, at that moment, a brisk wind whipped her hat from her head and sent it whirling down, down, impossibly down, like a child's paper helicopter.

*"Fantastique!"* a priest standing nearby said, snapping his fingers. *"Petite tournedos!"*

Elliott was noticing with surprise that the woman's hair, set free, was the same obstinate reddish hair, texture and tint, as Rory's—a genetic caprice he and Laura had never decoded, since no one in either family had ever had red or auburn hair.

The woman threw up her hands in a vain, far-too-late attempt to retrieve her hat as it sailed up and over.

"See?" she told Elliott, laughing. "No breeze, anywhere else, except for me! Does it serve me right? And now I have to walk *down*! And I hate the walking *down* more than the going up!"

"I'll walk in front of you, with my girls," Elliott offered. "Rory, my middle daughter, would walk on the parapet if I'd let her. And she could do it, too. She's a gymnast."

"She's a doll," the woman told him softly, as she turned to follow him to the mouth of the far too revealing staircase. "Except for her poor hair. Does she *hate* being a redhead?"

"Yes," Elliott said, "but everyone else thinks it's wonderful."

"Umm," the woman mused, "has she seen an orthodontist? She could have a partial retainer right now that might spare her a full set of braces later on. That should have been seen to sooner."

"I know, I know. I just have had so much to do for them . . . I let it slip. I'm a single parent."

"Her arch is small . . . ," the woman commented.

"Are you a dentist?" Elliott asked.

"Yes, I am," the woman told him. "I'm a children's dentist. Children are never afraid, you know. It's their parents who instill the fear." They proceeded into the line before the exit, when Elliott remembered the bag nestled in his pocket.

"I have to do something, so if you want to, you can go on," he suggested. "I'm sorry."

"What? Take a photo? I'll wait."

"Well, it's . . . embarrassing, a little private."

"Oh, I wouldn't want to . . . "

"It's my mother's ashes," Annie interrupted. "Well, some of them. She's dead. Well, obviously. And she always wanted to go to Paris with Dad; but instead she had a brain hemorrhage on the Big Dig, in Boston, in our car."

"The Big Dig? In Boston? Don't tell me they're still at that! I went to school in Boston," the woman said. "I live in the Berkshires."

"It was quite a long time ago," Elliott said.

"On Christmas Eve, it will be four years," Annie

corrected him. "That's not so long. She died at five o'clock at night. I was thirteen. I'll be seventeen in a month."

"Christmas?" The woman removed her sunglasses and covered her eyes with one hand. "That is what is unbearable about having a family. To love and let go. At least, that's how I comfort myself, because I've never had children, though I wanted them. My husband didn't. And then, I imagine I didn't want him, as a result. I'm talking too much. I always talk too much. But I suppose it's why I do the work I do. Not because I talk too much. Children. Being with children. I don't mean I can identify with your life. I would never suggest that not having something is the same as losing it. How unbearably sad. On Christmas?"

Elliott looked down and fiddled with his pockets, as if to cover up a shameful spot. "Yes," he admitted. "We go away at Christmas. To my father's in Florida. We've done okay. My mother-in-law virtually gave up her business to help out with the girls . . . we managed."

"Her heart went to a boy who was born with his heart backwards—not Grandma's, I mean my mom's.

He was twelve and he was on his last legs," Rory said, shooting Annie a triumphant look. "And her eyes went to a lady who'd never seen her baby. And her lungs . . ."

"That's okay, Rory, that's enough," Elliott told her gently.

"I'm impressed by that, all of that," the woman told Rory, seriously, without condescension. "She must have been a very remarkable woman."

"Not really," Rory said. "She could do back walkovers, even though she was an older lady, like you. She was nice, but Karen is a better cook, even Dad says so . . ."

"Your . . . girlfriend?" the woman asked Elliott, glancing at his left hand. He had removed his ring only two years before, on the night that Whitney, one of Laura's friends, arranged a date for him with one of the women who worked with her at her catering company. They'd had six dates. Elliott enjoyed her. Then, one day, when they were finishing a tennis match, the woman, Clare, a lively, compact brunette, tapped him on the rear with her racquet and told him, simply, she sensed that his heart wasn't in it—and Elliott knew she didn't mean the tennis.

"No, Karen is the woman who helps us out," Elliott explained, "at home. She is a great cook. She's worked for us since Laura died. Laura was more interested in the kids and the dog, in reading instead of cleaning. She did like to iron, but it took her all day to do two shirts. We didn't care. She could spend two hours making a giant macaroni mosaic with Amelia. And she *could* cook, Rory. Remember the Christmas cookies?"

"I remember the Christmas chocolate tree."

"See?" Annie said sharply. "You don't remember her. It's *called* a Bûche de Noel, Rory."

"No. None of you has forgotten her," the red-haired dentist interrupted. "Look what you're doing here. That matters. It's a lovely memorial. It's wonderful you're still mindful of her. And . . . if you don't care too much, I'll wait with you. All of you."

Elliott poured thimble-sized heaps of ash into each of the girls' hands. One by one, they opened their hands, brushing their palms as the sky darkened and the moon's ghostly crooked smile appeared. Elliott breathed slowly, out and in, then out again, no longer quite able to summon Laura's voice or her scent, but grateful he had kept a promise he had never believed he would keep, kept it through the good grace of Laura. Then he emptied the bag, blowing gently on the last particles, dispersing them in the dusk, until they disappeared into the first twinkling of nightfall in the City of Lights. Laura was in Paris.

"I'll walk down with you now," Elliott said, offering a handshake, forgetting, then blushing, drawing it back. "My hand may still have . . . I'm Elliott. *Je m'appelle* Elliott."

"That's all right," said the dentist, reaching out, taking his hand in a firm clasp. "I don't mind. I'm Amy."